DANGEROUS JOURNEY

DANGEROUS JOURNEY

A NOVEL

BY GLENN MATHEWS

1stBooks - re. 11/29/00

Dedication: To my darling Dee.

Chapter One

Sonoma, California. Late July, 1991.

Bruce Campbell had difficulty finding a parking space. The Village Shopping Center was busy. Pedestrians strolled the walkways in front of the shops. Adults would stop and examine window displays, and small children demanded attention. He slammed on the brakes, just ahead the back up lights of a station wagon indicated departure. He backed the Suburban a few yards and waited for the driver to back out and move forward.

The weather was hot with late morning humidity. Bruce lowered each of the four windows about three inches.

"You keep an eye on things, Christy," he said to the black Labrador in the backseat. "I might be awhile, and I don't want to hear you whining when I go."

The black Lab jumped over the back of the front seat and positioned herself behind the steering wheel. Christy looked slowly in all directions. She lay down on her master's seat and closed her eyes.

He locked the car doors and walked in the direction of the gift shop. Bruce Campbell was six feet tall and about ten pounds overweight at two hundred pounds. He had a full head of light gray hair parted on the right side and his hair was a little unruly, and long on the neck. He did not see a barber with regularity. He was sixty-one years old with hazel eyes, cheeks full but not fat, a hawk-like nose, and his lips were narrow and the teeth even. His legs, arms, and wide shoulders were still athletic looking, but the skin under his chin sagged a trifle and the stomach began to show signs of excess.

At the gift shop, Bruce examined the window displays critically and was pleased. Linen tablecloths, ceramic lamps, crystal vases and candlesticks, elaborate place mats, clocks, and kitchen accessories of all kinds were neatly arranged. The merchandise was quite beautiful and in some cases exquisite. He liked the name of the shop, 'Especially For You.' The business had an excellent location in the Center and was located on one of the corners of the walkway. Two other persons were looking at the gifts on display and he could see activity near the cash register. On the lower right corner of the window near the entrance, Bruce saw her name in gold lettering: 'Kathryn Stevens, Proprietor.' He went inside and was greeted by a blond Labrador that wagged its tail and wore a red kerchief with a snowflake design.

Bruce kneeled on one knee and patted the dog.

"Well, hello. You're very pretty, and what a pretty scarf you have on."

The dog seemed delighted.

"And she wears one for each day of the week, and her name is Sally. She's white but still considered a blond Lab." Bruce looked up and saw a young woman smiling at him.

Bruce stood.

"Hello, I'm here to buy a special gift. And I would like to see Ms. Stevens, if I may," he said quietly.

"Surely, but she's with customers right now. She will be a few moments," the young woman said.

"That's fine. I'm in no hurry. I'll look around in the meantime." Bruce showed interest in the glass case nearby, but he had looked quickly toward the cash register and saw the woman behind the counter. He hoped she was Kathryn Stevens.

The young woman went to the cash register. Her employer was busy wrapping a gift. "There's an older man by the plate section wanting to see you," she whispered. "And he likes your dog." The young woman pointed.

Kathryn Stevens looked in the direction indicated. "He's not an old man, Debra, but very distinguished looking. Beautiful gray hair."

"I didn't say old," Debra said, "I said older. And, I agree, he's not too shabby."

Bruce looked at a set of four crystal wine glasses. They were tall and thin stemmed. He read the price on a tiny tag, one hundred and fifty dollars. Sally remained sitting beside him, eager for attention.

"Hello, I'm Kathryn Stevens. May I help you?"

Bruce turned to see the woman behind the register. He looked into her dark brown eyes with the heavy but beautifully groomed natural eyebrows. Her brown hair was cut short, Dutch boy style. Her complexion was smooth and creamy. Rounded cheeks flowed to a firm concise chin, full sensuous lips, and a long elegant neckline. Her smile revealed even, white teeth. She was about five foot five or six and close to one hundred and twenty pounds. Her baggy white corduroy slacks and the loose fitting red blouse hid her figure. He estimated her age at mid-forty.

"Yes, I want to get a gift for good friends of mine." Bruce grinned. "I have my trailer parked on their driveway just a few blocks from here, and this isn't the first time. They've always been very kind to me."

"How much would you like to spend on the gift?" Kathryn seemed to be studying him.

"Well, not over fifty dollars if I can get something nice for that," Bruce said. "I liked these wine glasses but a hundred and fifty is too much for my blood. They are beautiful, and Jake, that's the husband, is a real connoisseur of wines. I'm not sure what Sam -- eh, Isabel, really likes." Bruce couldn't keep his eyes off Kathryn Stevens. He thought she was truly lovely.

"Are you talking about Jake and Sam Henderson?" she said.

"Yes, I guess the cat's out of the bag. They've been wanting us to get together on a blind date with them." Bruce tried to smile, this wasn't turning out the way he wanted.

"Are you the man that was divorced two or three years ago, and was married for --."

"Thirty-five years. That's me," he said.

"And you wanted to check the merchandise first?" She looked grim.

"Yes, I guess so." Bruce paused. He looked around the shop. There were no customers. The young woman had moved

3

from the cash register and inched toward them. He knew she was all ears. "I have to be honest. You're absolutely right, I did want to check the merchandise first." He paused. "You're quite lovely, and I'm very pleased."

There was another pause. He brightened.

"You know, it's a two way street."

She seemed to have difficulty keeping a straight face.

"If you please Sam, you will please Jake, and she likes to cook. Are you aware of that?"

"Yes, she bakes a lot," he said. "Cakes, cookies, pies. Why?"

She opened a box. "This cake or dessert plate just came in, and quite nice. High grade china, a harvest design, and made in Germany. Thirty-nine dollars. I'm sure Sam would be delighted."

Bruce looked casually at the plate. "I'm sure Sam would like it, and thank you for the suggestion, but not very special to Jake, and I would really like what I give to them. I guess fifty's not enough. Perhaps we should go higher."

"Nonsense," she said quickly. "Fifty dollars will buy a very thoughtful gift." She paused. "What do the three of you have in common?"

"Horse racing," he said. "We like to go to the races together. That's why I'm here. They invited me again to the Sonoma County Fair for two weeks of horse racing at Santa Rosa Fairgrounds. Jake always has reserved seats for the meet and pre-paid parking, and I go everyday, with or without them." He was impressed that she didn't want to get more money out of him.

"Let's go over there." She pointed to another glass case. She opened a drawer under the case and removed a larger box. One by one, she placed six highball glasses on the glass top. They were short, wide, thick glass, and on each was a racehorse running with a jockey.

4

"Made in Japan," she said. "Hand painted horse and jockey designs, good thick glass, not easily broken, and the set is known as 'The Champions'. You will note that --."

"I see, I see," he interrupted. "The actual portraiture of the horse with the owner's colors." His enthusiasm was evident as he read the small print under each horse. "John Henry, Secretariat, Affirmed, Alysheba, Man O' War, Count Fleet. I'll take it. I'll take it. We all drink a highball once in a while you know. Just perfect. Can I get it gift wrapped?"

"Of course." She smiled happily.

The dog's tail wagged and slapped against her corduroys.

"Sally even approves!" She placed the glasses in the box and walked with them toward the cash register.

He followed her closely and examined her behind. No evidence of figure. "I'm very pleased. Thank you, Kathryn."

She had reached the cash register when he had spoken her name. She turned toward him. "I don't need to be thanked, Mister Campbell. I'm glad that you're pleased."

"I didn't mean to be forward by calling you Kathryn. I guess I just said it naturally. I've heard Sam refer to you as Kathryn so many times." He saw that the young woman was getting gift paper and ribbon from under the counter. He assumed she hadn't missed a word of their conversation. He didn't care, but the dinner invitation had to be private.

"Actually, I would prefer calling you Kate, if you don't mind. And my name is Bruce." He held out his hand.

She took his hand, not shaking, just a light pressure from her.

"I think I would like that --, Bruce," she said. "Only one other person has called me Kate, a girlfriend in high school. We were close friends. She was a rambunctious person with an infectious laugh. Are you rambunctious, Bruce?" She looked at him and smiled.

"No longer, age and bypass surgery have a tendency to slow one down," he said. He thought it strange to admit to the beginnings of antiquity when meeting someone, but he didn't care. There was something about this woman. Something that made him feel that he should always level with her. "Although my English teacher in high school referred to me as an exuberant clown, but that was a long time ago." He laughed and removed his wallet.

"The glasses are forty-seven dollars and fifty cents, plus tax. The total will be a little higher than you intended to spend."

He handed her a fifty and a five dollar bill. "I couldn't be more pleased."

He bent down to pet Sally. The dog had waited patiently for more attention. Bruce got on both knees and hugged her.

"My, what a wiggle tail. How old are you?"

"Six years, going on one," Kate said. "She's a character and always into something, but I love her."

"Christy, my black Lab, is eleven, but she's active and still quite strong. Has to play ball everyday." He knew now was the time to try and get her out of the shop. "Would you like to see her? She's in my Suburban."

There was silence for a few moments. His purchase was nicely gift wrapped, placed in a plastic bag with loop handles, and his change was returned to him. He felt his heart beating rapidly.

"Yes, I'd like that." She turned to Debra. "Watch Sally, and hold it down for a few minutes?"

"Gladly," Debra took a deep breath.

They went outside and walked toward his vehicle. He immediately directed her into the big parking lot.

"You have a great location in a busy and attractive center," he said. "What do you pay for rent?"

He felt her stillness. He looked at her and saw her expression.

"I know," he said, "it's none of my damn business. You'll have to excuse me but I was in real estate for twenty-four years in Tahoe. I had my own business which was sold in the spring of eighty-six. I managed a lot of properties, all types of property management. I was just naturally interested, particularly with the apparent activity in this Center on a weekday. You have about eight hundred and fifty square feet which includes the small rest room and some storage. Right?"

"Eight hundred and sixty-seven square feet to be exact. I pay nine hundred per month plus my pro-rated share of taxes on the Center, plus utilities. The owner pays for refuse and water. My rent can increase annually based on the Standard of Living Index. Any more questions?" She smiled at him.

"That's very reasonable. I would say you have the best location in this shopping area." They reached the yellow Suburban.

"Here we are." He unlocked the front door and Christy greeted them happily.

Kate immediately hugged the dog, and her attentions were received warmly. Christy's tail slapped her shoulders, head and upper torso.

"Oh, Bruce, she's a beauty. What a nice dog. And her hair, so glossy and soft. What do you do to keep her in such wonderful condition?"

He was pleased. "Two tablespoons of safflower oil in her food twice a month will keep her coat shiny and soft. Perfect weight, sixty-three pounds. She gets a vitamin everyday. She's showing signs of age though. Note the gray hair on her underbelly, bottom, chin, and paws. She's slowing down a little, but not much." He talked rapidly and he didn't want to discuss the dog. He wanted to ask her out but he felt awkward about it. Forty years had elapsed since he asked a woman for a date.

"I would like very much to take you to dinner, Kate," he said. "Perhaps you're free one night this week. How about tomorrow night?" he blurted.

"Not tomorrow night," she said casually. "But the next evening would be fine if you're free."

"Yes, fine." Relief was very evident in his voice. "I don't know Sonoma or its restaurants that well. Would you pick the place and time?"

7

Glenn Mathews

"All right. Pick me up this Thursday evening at seven and we'll walk to Marioni's in the Village Square, just three blocks from my house." She gave him her address.

With pen in hand he scribbled her address on an old business card in his wallet.

"Walk?" he said. "Why walk? I don't like walking. And it's chilly here in the evening. Can't we take the Suburban?"

"No." She seemed adamant. "You won't find a parking spot in the Square this time of year. And, I like walking. I walk everyday or evening, or both. And the exercise will do you no harm."

"You sound awfully bossy," he quipped, "but I'll give it a try." He looked at his watch. "I'm meeting Jake in about five minutes. We're going to the races at the Fair." He had to leave but he wanted her to be comfortable about his sudden departure. "I'm really looking forward to Thursday evening."

Kate laughed. "I can take a hint." She patted Christy again, and started walking toward her business. "See you at seven on Thursday," she said over her shoulder. "Goodbye for now."

"Goodbye, Kate."

He got in the Suburban and started the engine. He sat there and watched her walk. Kate had placed her hands in her pants pockets which tightened the fabric over her buttocks. "She does have a good-looking ass, Christy. She does."

Kate reached the gift shop, held the door open for departing customers, and went inside to an anxious looking Debra. She avoided the look and found activity by putting the pie plate back in its box and placing it in a drawer.

"Come on, Kathryn," Debra said, "don't be mum. What did he say? Did he invite you out?"

"Yes."

"You accepted, of course."

"It wasn't that easy. But, yes, I accepted." Kate looked at her assistant. "That man needs a woman to talk to. He needs to be understood. He needs some kindness, and I think I can help."

8

"Help? Kindness?" Debra said in seeming disbelief. "A good-looking sexy man, probably highly intelligent, with a bedroom voice, asks you out. And all you can think of is talk or kindness?"

Kate was pensive. She remembered the havoc to her shop two years ago. Everyone thought it was general vandalism. No one knew the real cause. No one ever would. "Yes, Debra," she said, "that's all I can think of, or do. Just talk and be kind."

Chapter Two

They returned from dinner on the Village Square, walking to Kate's home. The Village Square consists of four blocks, each block the side of a square, and having small retail businesses, restaurants, and older hotels. The improvements are old but well maintained. Attractive alleyways leave the sidewalk intriguing the visitor, and introducing other colorful stores. In the center of the Village Square is the Village Park, its center the city hall. The park is practical and attractive. Wide walkways next to lawns, rose gardens, stone bridges over duck ponds, playgrounds, and an outside theater were well placed. The ducks are plentiful and usually in groups. A city ordinance gives them the right of way, including crossing the busy streets.

The shortcut through the Village Park would normally have been enjoyable but the evening was cool, and dampness hung in the air. Kate wore a knee length white skirt, a blue blouse, a white cardigan cashmere sweater, and low heeled white shoes. Bruce wore a long sleeved blue plaid shirt, dark slacks, and black Hush Puppies. He had counted the number of blocks to the restaurant from Kate's home and discovered the distance to be five blocks rather than the expected three blocks. The air was colder on their return and he was uncomfortable. He was also upset that he had not worn a jacket. He could not believe that California weather could be this cold in late July. He tried to hide his emotions from Kate but he had failed.

"You're not enjoying yourself," she said. "We should have driven, there was a parking spot after all. I'm sorry to have been so insistent. I enjoy walking and I forget that there are people who don't like to walk, or exercise in any manner."

"You can count me as one of them. I've done my share and I've never liked it," Bruce said. "I'm sorry to be a party pooper. I feel like an old man who wants an electric blanket wrapped around him."

She laughed, and he enjoyed her laughter. "Sixty-one is not old, Bruce. You just think you are."

They approached her home and could see the slight movement of Christy behind the steering wheel.

"Bring your dog in now," Kate said. "Let's see how the two of them are together."

Kate went to unlock the side door while Bruce got the dog. Christy seemed apprehensive, as if she knew there was a dog in there. The entrance led into the family room and Sally greeted her mistress. She sat and inspected the black dog. She showed no alarm. There was no sniffing. Christy walked past the blond Lab with disinterest. The exception was her low menacing growl.

"Cut that crap out," Bruce exclaimed. "You are the guest, Christy, and act like it!"

He went to the fireplace and placed two logs from the hearth on the low embers. He appreciated what warmth there was, but hoped the new logs would ignite quickly. He sat on the hearth near the firebox.

Christy inspected the house.

"She's going to look into every nook and cranny," Bruce said.

"What else can you expect from a real estate dog?" Kate said from the kitchen. "You inspected everything when you arrived. Pretty gutsy, I thought. Particularly when you went into my walk-in closet in my bedroom!"

"I just can't help myself," he laughed. "You do have a very nice home. The house has a good-looking Cape Cod front elevation, but there is some functional obsolescence in the interior." He knew he was showing off. "Limited storage and closet space and this family room is on the small side. Placing furniture is a problem, and the room crowds the dinette area. Average construction, and built in 1963 if we're to believe the imprinted date on the bottom of the water closet cover." He went on, sounding like a brochure.

Sally came and placed her head on his lap, and he patted her.

11

"From what little I know of value in the area," he said, "this house is worth about three hundred thousand dollars."

Kate brought a tray of coffee and chocolate cake. She set the tray on the coffee table between the two small leather sofas in front of the fireplace.

"Did you expect me to pay you for your detailed and knowledgeable appraisal of my home? You are one critical son of a bitch. Aren't you?" She sat down on one of the sofas and crossed her legs. "I feel like you invaded my home." She laughed.

He noted her good-looking legs with the smoke colored hosiery. "I won't charge for the appraisal, it's a freebie. And, yes, I am very critical, and I intimidate, too.

"And I'm told that I dominate people and situations," he said slowly. He was thoughtful for several moments. "We both wanted a divorce, but these characteristics of mine were the main reasons Elizabeth wanted the divorce. There were other reasons."

"Would you like to talk about the divorce, and Elizabeth?" Kate said kindly. "I would be interested if you want to."

He looked at her and he knew that she had removed his mask. His aggressive behavior was merely a front, a cover up. He was comfortable with her at dinner. Once he returned to her home, he did not know how to act, or what was expected of him. He felt like he didn't know how to be with a woman anymore. There was never a problem in high school and college, but age and a long disappointing marriage made a difference.

Christy had finished the house inspection and returned to the family room.

Bruce finished his coffee, and stood. The fireplace was getting hot, and he went to the sofa across from Kate.

Sally decided to lay at her feet.

Christy sat by his legs, then plopped down, her right paw on the master's foot. She moaned and emitted a very quiet growl at the dog across from her.

"Yes," he said, "I would like to talk about the divorce. To try and explain the why of it all. I don't know where to begin."

"At the beginning," Kate said. "Where did you meet Elizabeth?"

"In the student cafeteria on the campus at UCLA," he began. "We were both between classes. There was a vacant chair next to her and I sat down with my lunch. I spilled milk on her, and–, we started seeing each other. She was a sophomore, I was a junior, a transfer from San Mateo Junior College. She was a very pretty young lady. Small, only five feet. Blond, and about a hundred pounds. She was a good dancer and had an engaging personality. Despite the draft --" Bruce paused, and smiled cynically. "In those days the war was referred to as the Korean Conflict. I was able to maintain a B average and graduate in nineteen-fifty-one. I didn't want to be drafted. Before enlisting I passed the army's verbal and written requirements for officer's training and was assured of candidacy. My basic training was at Fort Ord, near Monterey, and O.T.S. was at Fort Benning, Georgia. Liz and I saw each other on occasional weekends during my initial months of enlistment and training when I had a pass."

He reached for his chocolate cake and began to nibble, not knowing its taste. "Once she came to Georgia for a week prior to my graduation. We were in love and she wanted to get married immediately, but we waited awhile longer. I requested further training as a field agent in the Counter Intelligence Corps when I became a second lieutenant. My request was granted and training was at Fort Holobird, Maryland. I had a thirty day pass when I left Holobird and Liz and I were married in West Los Angeles right after her graduation in nineteen-fifty-two." Bruce stopped and stared at the fireplace.

Moments passed.

"And then what happened?" Kate gently said.

He continued to stare.

"Bruce?" she said louder.

13

Glenn Mathews

He looked at Kate, and his face relaxed. "I'm sorry, my mind drifts these days." He gathered his thoughts, and smiled. "We spent our honeymoon finding an apartment and furnishing it with used furniture. We found a nice one bedroom apartment in a triplex on North Palm Drive in Beverly Hills for seventy-five dollars per month. Can you imagine that?"

"No, I can't." Kate laughed.

"I was assigned to Army Headquarters in Seoul, Korea, and Liz got a job as a service representative at the Pacific Telephone Company in Beverly Hills. I didn't see Liz again for fifteen months."

He stopped again. His jaw tightened, and hate appeared on his face. "What a terrible fifteen months. So much deceit and treachery. So much killing, and you didn't have to wear a uniform either. There were over eight million people in Seoul."

He became pensive again. "The city is on the Han River, a nice place to hide something, or someone." He reached for his coffee mug, not realizing it was empty. He tried to concentrate on the chocolate cake. "Killing another person is quite awful."

Kate took the tray into the kitchen and heated the coffeepot. She returned to the family room and handed him a mug. "Now drink it while it's hot."

"Thank you." He took several sips of the hot coffee. "I was shot in the side by a KGB agent. Fortunately, I was still able to kill him. After a few weeks in an army hospital in Seoul I was sent stateside to recuperate and take the leave which had accumulated. Looking back, I think this was the happiest time in our married lives. Liz and I were very happy. We were always laughing and talking together. It was a fun time, and I felt secure and safe. Hell, I was only twenty-three, but after Korea, I was going on forty. I stayed in the service for another eleven years, and we moved near Arlington, Virginia, where we bought a small but nice home. In 1961, our oldest son, David, was born there. I eventually became a Major and often worked out of the Pentagon. I spent considerable time at CIA headquarters in Langley, Virginia, helping to train their field agents. The army

14

had sort of leased me out to the CIA because of my experience, and I learned later that the Agency specifically requested me. After all, I had a reputation as a legitimate paid killer. I was thankful that I never went back into the actual espionage world. So much secrecy. Death, torture, distrust, intrigue, blackmail, exchange of information or people, all were quite common, and I got tired of playing my part."

He became thoughtful again. "And I was saddened and frustrated with the death of John Kennedy," he said quietly. "Also, with Johnson, we knew our forces in Vietnam would multiply, and the war would escalate. I left the army in nineteen-sixty-four, and the three of us went to South Lake Tahoe, California. Liz and I had been to Tahoe a couple of times on vacation and I thought at the time that both of us really liked Tahoe. I worked as a salesman in real estate for a couple of years, studied for my broker's license and passed the test. I opened my own office in nineteen-sixty-seven, and I guess that became the beginning of the end to our marriage. We were foolish. We never should have stayed married for another twenty years."

Sally went to the rear door of the family room. Christy joined her.

"Time for the dogs to go out," Kate said. "Anyway, Sally has to go this time of night."

Both dogs barked excitedly as the door opened, and they raced over the redwood deck, down its steps, and into the dark recesses of the backyard. They continued to bark.

Kate turned on the light over the deck and went outside to wait for the dogs. "Stop that barking," she said.

Bruce joined her. "A nice yard, what I can see of it. Not too big, just enough."

"The yard needs lots of work. My plants and roses are pooping out. I don't have the time for the yard anymore."

The dogs returned. Sally wanted in immediately, Christy looked at her master. Once inside, Sally went to the downstairs bedroom.

"She's going to her bed in my bedroom. It's that time of night," Kate said.

"Yes, it is, and we'll get going too," Bruce said. "I've done all the talking. I'm sorry."

"You're not going anywhere." Kate smiled. "Sit down on that sofa again, and tell me the reasons for the divorce. And I was very interested hearing you talk about yourself. More coffee?"

"No, thank you."

After following Sally into the bedroom, Christy returned to the family room, lay down next to her master, and again placed a paw on his foot, and closed her eyes.

"Steven," Bruce said. "Our second son and last child, was born in nineteen-sixty-seven, the same year I opened my office. Business was very good until nineteen-eighty. Liz designed the new home we'd built. A beautiful home on nearly an acre of land that overlooked a large meadow and part of the Truckee River. I became too involved. I was on the planning commission, the chamber of commerce, Rotary Club, and various committees, in addition to the sixty hours per week on the job. I neglected my family. They had most anything they wanted except a husband and a father. The boys grew up without me."

Bruce stood and went to the hearth, and stared at the flames. "Oh, we took the annual vacations and went to many interesting and beautiful places," he said. "And I always took one month off when school was out. But that wasn't enough. I would get home at night, very tired, have my dinner, and doze off watching TV from the sofa. I have only myself to blame really. I'm a very critical person. I guess I expect a lot of people or things, and so did Liz. There was an argument almost every day in our marriage. We argued about the boys usually, or money."

He sat again. "We never agreed. For over twenty years, Liz never said 'I love you.'"

Tears formed in his eyes, and he continued slowly. "She never reached for my hand. She never initiated a hug. Our sex life was always poor, but there was no sex the last several years of our marriage. Neither of us missed it. Yet, we were loyal to one another. That I'm sure of. There was never any possessiveness or jealousy. We trusted each other completely, but we didn't get along. Oh, Liz wanted to discuss these problems, constantly. But the discussions would develop into accusations, yelling and arguing. Eventually, I spent my evenings in the den."

Bruce got up and walked around the family room. He sat next to Kate. "Oh, Liz was a damn good mother," he said. "She was always attentive to her sons. Always making sure that they had what they needed, or wanted, and she was there when they needed someone to talk to. I was aware that I ran a damn poor second in her affections. She did a good job. I'm very proud of my sons and I love them very much. I am sure they know that. I've told them." Bruce stopped talking. He stared at nothing.

"How would you like a damn good glass of wine," Kate interrupted his thoughts. She stood and walked quickly toward the kitchen. "I won't take no for an answer!"

A tear had fallen on her cheek. She reached for the paper towels and tore two sheets from the rack. She dampened the sheets under the kitchen faucet and wiped her face. She held the towels on her face for several moments. She placed two large wine glasses on the coffee tray, took ice from the freezer and dropped a cube into each glass. She removed a half bottle of white wine from the refrigerator and placed the bottle on the tray removing the previously opened cork by hand.

She returned to the family room. "If you don't like this wine, you shouldn't drink wine," Kate laughed. "It's an excellent local table wine that's very reasonable. Besides, the couple that owns this winery come into my shop all the time. They're very good customers, and I do have to reciprocate." She poured a good amount of wine into each glass, and then sat again, next to him.

Bruce smiled at her, reached for his glass and drank several sips. "It is good wine. Thank you."

17

Glenn Mathews

"You told me earlier that you sold your business in nineteen-eighty-six. Is that correct?" Kate said.

"Yes. Liz never liked living in Tahoe. What with the casino environment at Stateline, she referred to it 'as the drug capital of the world.' The boys have told me several times that they felt lucky having grown up in Tahoe. So many outdoor activities, and the area is quite beautiful, but business was no longer beautiful. In nineteen-eighty, the recession began all over the country, and interest rates became extremely high. Eventually, most of the country adjusted, but not Tahoe. For years, real estate sales were poor. The vacation home, or the secondary home market, was the basic real estate attraction in Tahoe, but then it suffered. Tax laws changed, and it was no longer an advantage to write off a vacation home that was rented, and interest rates remained high. The buyer had no great need to buy a vacation home. He could wait until things got better."

He patted Christy, and he drank more wine, enjoying its taste. "Consequently, my income really suffered and I had to go in another direction, property management. Tahoe is always a great vacationland, and I acquired excellent vacation rentals, and monthly rentals. The workers at the Stateline casinos normally rented. My rental commissions soared, and gradually sale commissions got better. I had something to sell in nineteen-eighty-six, and Liz wanted out of Tahoe."

Bruce finished his wine. "By then, the boys had left Tahoe. Dave got his master's degree and a good job in Southern California with a consulting firm that specializes in administrative and management problems affecting local and county governments. Dave's a great kid. He's stubborn as a mule, but a very thoughtful kind person. He and Jan have been married for five years now, and I have a four year old grandson."

He paused for several moments. "When I sold the business, Steve was a junior in college at Davis. It was just Liz and I living in a big house. We sold the house and the business, purchased the trailer I'm living in, and traveled. Then, we spent all our waking hours together, hoping that our marriage would

18

improve, but it didn't, matters just got worse. We didn't like each other. There was no love."

Bruce got up and added another log to the fireplace. He returned to the sofa. "Our divorce was final in the fall of eighty-seven. We split down the middle what money and assets were left. She's living with her sister in the Bay Area now, and apparently likes her job in an arts and crafts store." He was quiet for a few moments. "It's a terrible thing to say," he said calmly. "But I don't really care what she does. I have no animosity. I wish her well. But I don't ever want to see her again."

There was a long pause. "What does Steve do now?" Kate said.

"He works for a large investment firm in the Los Angeles area," Bruce said. "He loves the business world. I hope one day he'll meet a nice girl, if he can ever find time for something other than the stock market and mutual funds. He's a very intelligent young man."

"Do the brothers get along?"

"Yes, but they argue quite a bit. Over nothing, really," Bruce said. "They love each other. I hope so, anyway."

"At dinner, you said you settled near Tiller, Oregon." Kate sipped her wine.

"Yes, population three hundred, if you count the people ten miles in any direction from Tiller," Bruce said. "I rent an RV pad with full hookups on an acre of land by the South Umpqua River. Very private, very primitive, very beautiful. The owners are good friends of mine from UCLA days, and they've been very kind to me, trying to help me get my life going again. I have no neighbors, just me and Christy, and the wild life that I enjoy. There's a tiny market a block away called 'The Last Frontier.'" He laughed. "I didn't settle there until the fall of eighty-nine, after my surgery. I'm comfortable there, and content now. It's my home. I have excellent satellite television, and a great view. I read. I fish. I've trimmed or removed tons of brush and trees, and have a great yard going. I've even started a novel about horse racing. What the hell, I keep busy. And I get

19

Glenn Mathews

to Sonoma once in awhile, and to Southern California to visit the boys and Santa Anita Race Track."

"What about your surgery, Bruce? What happened? Do you mind telling me?" Kate said.

"Not at all. Again, I was fortunate to have good friends. I was here for the Fair about this time in eighty-nine and parked the rig at Jake and Sam's house. We visit almost every night in their home. You know, of course, that Jake is an internist, and he was expressing concern one evening that I didn't look well. I had to admit that I was experiencing some chest pain and discomfort in my upper arms. Well, Jake immediately arranged for me to see a heart specialist and surgeon in Santa Rosa. In less than three days I had a double bypass." He saw the concern and sympathy on Kate's face. "No big deal, bypass surgery is common now, and I feel good."

Kate removed the tray from the coffee table.

He followed her into the kitchen.

"Don't underestimate your surgery," Kate said. "You take care of yourself."

"I take care of myself," he said quietly. "I really feel lucky about my home by the river. I found out about it when my friends, Tom and Lois Ackerman, visited me in the hospital. They live in Whittier and were on their way to Oregon and Washington for a vacation. Tom told me the RV pad was vacant and mine if I wanted it." He waited several moments. "So there you have it," he said. "My life story, and I've been yacking all night."

He sat on the chair in the kitchen and watched her. "May I ask a question about your ex-husband?"

She placed the wine glasses and dessert dishes into the dishwasher. "Let's not get into that tonight. It's late, and the topic is one that I dislike."

"Is he Mafia?" he said. "That's what Sam heard."

"Yes," she said after several moments.

"How long were you married to him?"

"Twenty-two years."

20

"Any good years with him?"

"None. Any more questions?" She sounded angry.

"One more."

"That's all I'm going to give you. Just one more," she said. "I've had a very pleasant evening. Let's not spoil it."

"Why did you stay married so long?" he said.

"I didn't expect you to ask a question like that," Kate said. "Why did you stay married for thirty-five years? Because you were foolish, you said. You both stayed married for the well being of your sons, if they were better off. The twins were one of the reasons I stayed married. Originally, I felt an obligation. Then I became scared and frightened. I thought he would hurt me or the children if I left him."

He wanted to ask other questions, but he didn't. Instead, he took both her hands in his.

"I've had a wonderful evening," he said. "And, somehow, I feel better. Relieved, if you will. Thank you."

He continued to look into her eyes. "May I call you soon?" he said.

"I would be disappointed if you didn't," Kate said.

Two hours later, in an area known as Hillsborough, an old man was being helped to bed. Hillsborough, on the Peninsula and twenty miles south of San Francisco, is a community for the very wealthy. An area of estates, not merely houses. Manicured lawns, thick foliage, curved driveways, and meticulous care prevailed. Privacy and seclusion were imperative. The old man had retired much earlier but the need to urinate was frequent. He was of medium height, almost bald, hawk like features, with eyes that had sunken from loss of weight. He was sickly and frail and partially paralyzed on his left side. His mind was still alert and always active. He was helped from the wheelchair onto an enormous bed that complimented an enormous room, part bedroom and part sitting room. The expensive furniture was heavy and ornate.

"Has Charlie returned?" the old man said to his Filipino valet and bodyguard.

The Filipino was a large man, middle aged, a head of thick black hair, a rounded face with smooth facial features. The body was strong, muscular, and well trained. His clothing never changed when he cared for his employer: black shoes and socks, black gabardine slacks, and a white short sleeved silk shirt, open at the neck.

He had lifted the old man from the wheelchair and placed him easily and gently on the bed, covering him with a sheet and two thin blankets.

"Yes, sir, he just came in when I responded to your buzzer. I think he's in the kitchen getting something to eat."

"Get him."

"Yes, sir."

Charlie Dobbs had been with his employer for fifteen years. He was reliable, careful, and accurate. The old man paid him very well, and a bonus was paid frequently. He never questioned the reasons for his instructions. He just did what he was told to do, and he did it very well. He was not quite forty and he was in very good physical condition. He exercised daily in addition to weight lifting. He maintained a dark tan. He was six foot, no fat, bald on the top of his head, and he had a pockmarked face that was heavily lined. He ate a sandwich of pumpernickel and cheese and drank a glass of skim milk when Roy, the Filipino, came into the kitchen.

"He wants to see you."

Charlie stood and left the kitchen. He went up the wide staircase to the second floor and to the double doors opposite the landing. He opened the door on the right side, went into the room and closed the door. He went to within a few feet of the bed, stood casually, with his hands folded in front of him.

"Did they fuck?" the old man said.

"No, Mister Moroni, they had dinner and just talked," Charlie said. "They walked from her home to a restaurant on the square, were there about an hour and a half, and then they walked to her home and had some dessert and coffee, wine later, and talked for a couple of hours. He didn't even kiss her goodnight. He could have been her brother."

"How do you know they didn't go to bed?"

"I saw them," Charlie said. "I went around to the street behind them and into the backyard that's next to her backyard. I had my binoculars on her rear window. She never draws the drapes until she goes to bed. They were always in the family room or the kitchen. The Labs came out to crap, and barked at me, but she thought they were just having fun."

"I want them watched. I want to know what they're doing when they're together. If I need you for something else, put Smitty or Roy on it." He still had a strong voice.

"Yes, Mister Moroni."

Charlie left the room and returned to the kitchen.

Chapter Three

The Sonoma County Fair had closed. The last day of horse racing was the previous Sunday. Bruce would leave tomorrow and return to his home in Oregon. There was a lot of work waiting for him there. During the last twelve days, he and Kate had been together on five occasions. They were the initial dinner engagement, two luncheons, dinner at her home, and now tonight, another home cooked meal and an introduction to her father, a widower.

Stanley Stevens was a small man, about five foot seven, and wiry. Heavy and black eyebrows emphasized a weathered face with sharp wrinkled features and dark brown eyes. He had a salt and pepper crew cut above a high forehead that almost promised baldness. He was seventy-five years old, aging well, and retired, having worked as a plumber.

Bruce liked Stanley immediately. They had a common interest, fishing, although their methods were different. They were sitting outside drinking bourbon highballs while Kate barbecued spareribs on the patio.

"I am not going to hike up and down a riverbank casting out a fly line all the time," Bruce insisted. "Give me a nice deep pool of water and a shady rock to sit on, and I'm content having my line in the water with a tasty night crawler on it."

"That's no way to fish!" Stanley Stevens said. "There's no sport involved sitting on your ass!"

"I'm comfortable, I'm relaxed, and I enjoy myself," Bruce said. "I don't need to get my feet wet, stumble over rocks, or hike with a rod in my hand. Pass!"

"And you expect me to come up there and go fishing with you?" Stanley said.

"Yes! You hike and fly cast all you want. In addition to the river there are lots of creeks to investigate and wear yourself out in the doing. Just let me squat!"

They laughed. The two men enjoyed each other. The topic changed to gardening and Bruce became very attentive. He liked to garden and he wanted to know more on the care of roses and camellias and Stanley knew a great deal about them. Stanley had brought his daughter three branches filled with the most beautiful white camellias Bruce had ever seen. And he brought a bouquet of roses that were gorgeous and smelled like expensive perfume.

"You bring this daughter of mine to my home for dinner one night," Stanley said. "And I'll give you some sprigs and cuttings from my better camellias and roses. I'll tell you how to plant them and they'll do just fine in Oregon. I have a really fine rose called 'Glory Days'. It's pink, perfect petal formation, and keeps its shape for several days when cut." He paused, and laughed. "You don't even have to bring my daughter."

"Thanks, Stan, I just might do that," Bruce said. He looked at Kate hoping for some sign of her acceptance to the invitation but she avoided his look.

She finished cooking the ribs that were stacked on a large plate.

"Let's go inside," she said. "The salad is made and I'll get the potatoes and biscuits out of the oven. I've cooked some cauliflower, too. Dad, you get the wine and salad out of the refrigerator, and get some glasses and ice. Bruce, you sit at the table and stay out of our way. Dinner is going to be served and you guys better eat!"

They ate and when they were getting full they ate some more. There was one rib left on the platter, each eyed the rib and then each other. Kate stabbed the meaty part with her fork and rushed it to her plate. "Cry your heart out guys," she said. "Wish I had some more, but I don't."

"I'm the guest," Bruce said. "You realized that, didn't you?"

"Tough," she said.

"And I'm the oldest, your father," Stanley said, "and needed the extra nourishment."

Glenn Mathews

"Tough," she said. The rib was devoured and the bare bone dropped on her dinner plate. "Very good if I say so myself."

They all laughed.

"All the dinner was good," Stanley said. "I really believe you're as good a cook as your mother. Maybe even better!"

"No," Kate said. "I learned all the cooking goodies from Mom, but she was the master." She glanced quickly at her father.

The dogs waited at the rear door. Each had begged quietly during the meal but dinner was over. Kate left the table and opened the door. The Labs went through a rubber dog opening, a flap installed on the lower corner of the screen door leading to the rear patio and yard. Christy quickly and happily adapted to this readily available exit and entrance.

Kate returned to the dinner table . "You know, Dad, you should live here. There's plenty of room. You'd have a bedroom and bath all for yourself. This yard needs your touch. You'd be kept busy. You could sell or rent the San Mateo property. You and I get along real well, and Sally would like you to come, too. And, home cookin' all the time!"

Stanley smiled. "I love you, kid, and I appreciate what you are offering but, hell, that's no way for us to live. Each of us needs our own way of living and our own home. I get by real well, and I can cook, too, you know." He paused. "I sure need to see you and Sally once in a awhile, kid, and stay a few days, but not every day, day in and day out. Besides, I need to be where your mother was for so many years. I see her everywhere, and I enjoy that." He placed his hand on hers and saw the tears in his daughter's eyes, and the understanding. He looked at Bruce and saw the gentle smile. He understood, too.

They heard the rubber flap on the screen door. A low growl emanated from Christy as she trotted to her master. She looked at Bruce with fear and insistence in her eyes. She barked harshly and went to the screen door.

"Come on, something's wrong," Bruce said. He walked quickly to the backyard. Kate and her father followed him.

26

Sally lay in a heap near the rear fence. An arrow penetrated her chest. The metal tip of the arrow had exited behind her right elbow. She lay on her left side, her glazed eyes half open. She was alive. She breathed in short, quick spurts. The ground under her rib cage was soaked with blood. Christy lay upright, her front paws and nose extended. They touched her friend's nose and mouth. She whined in sympathy. The tip of Sally's tail moved slightly.

Stanley reached to remove the arrow.

"Don't do that!" Bruce yelled. "She'd bleed to death! Kate, go and call your vet. Now! Tell him we're coming. I'll take care of her and get her into the Suburban."

Bruce looked at Kate and he could tell that she was going into shock. He placed his hands on her shoulders and shook her vigorously.

"Get your head out of your ass, Kate, and call your vet! We might just save her."

Anger and hate were in Kate's eyes. She turned quickly and ran toward the house. Stanley stayed with the dogs when Bruce went to the Suburban to pull a blanket off the rear seat. He ran back and covered Sally, gently lifting her rump and left side to push the blanket under and around her body. He was careful not to touch the arrow. Blood slowly oozed from the wounds. As he picked the dog up he noticed three small dog treats on the bloody ground where the body had been.

Bruce walked quickly toward the Suburban. "Stan, open the rear door behind the driver's seat. I'll place the dog on her left side and Kate can sit beside her. You sit up front with me." He carefully placed the dog over seams that were coming apart on the seat. "There now, Sally, you just go ahead and bleed. You're not going to hurt old George here, he's been around a long time. Old George is the Suburban, you know. Christy and I call him George."

Sally whimpered. She didn't move when Kate sat next to her. Bruce opened the tailgate. Christy jumped in and placed her head on the back of the rear seat over Sally.

Glenn Mathews

The veterinarian allowed Kate to be in surgery. Kate seemed determined to be with her dog, to see Sally through this or be with her when she died. Bruce and her father were in the reception area.

"Did you see the dog bones?" Bruce said.

"Yes, but I didn't need to see them to know what happened."

"What the hell does that mean?" Bruce looked at Stanley with disbelief. "I don't know what the hell is going on here. The dog didn't hurt anybody! Surely, no one would deliberately hurt a dog."

"No one but Moroni," Stanley said quietly.

"What about Moroni?"

The older man studied Bruce's face. "Kate hasn't told you then?" He received no response. "It's up to Kate to tell you. I"m not going to."

"Tell me what? Goddamn it, your daughter is hiding something from her past and it's affecting our relationship. It needs telling, Stan." There was no reply.

"I think I love your daughter," Bruce said softly. "But there's something there, something standing in the way. We need each other. If I know anything, I know we need each other." There was no response. Stanley had picked up a magazine and glanced through it.

"You loved Kate's mother and you love the memory of her. Give me that same chance. Give me the chance to love your daughter." No response. "For Christ's Sake, man, what's going on around here?"

The magazine was lowered.

"She's afraid you're going to be hurt," Stanley said soberly. "And I am not talking about feelings."

"I can take care of myself." Bruce thought a moment. "What the hell, once I know what's going on, and I feel like it, I can run like hell. Bye, bye, baby!"

Stanley saw the smile and he laughed. "Alright, I'll tell you what I know." He became pensive for several moments. "Vincent Moroni is Kate's ex-husband."

28

"I know that."

"There's a helluva' lot you don't know," Stanley said. "He's the bottom of the barrel. Slime. Powerful, and worth millions, but his character isn't worth a nickel. If he felt he needed to, he would harm or kill anybody, except Kate. He thinks he still loves her, knows she doesn't love him, yet he doesn't want any other man to love her. He's older than I am and he's determined to make Kate's life miserable. He wouldn't harm Kate physically, just emotionally. Gets his kicks that way. So, he attacks her by hurting those who become close to her, including a dog. Hell, I'm surprised he hasn't tried to kill me."

"He's a fucking animal!"

"You're not being kind to the Sallys and Christys in this world," Stanley said. "Kate married the bastard when she was twenty-three. The twins, Edward and Karen, were born a year later. Great kids. They have no use for their father and they're making it on their own. They love their mother dearly and he's aware of that which only adds fuel to the fire. About the time their divorce was final, over four years ago, Moroni had a stroke. He lost the use of his legs and blames Kate and the divorce for his condition. He's always got to blame something on someone." Stanley shook his head. "Piss poor husband, father, and an asshole!"

"Kate didn't have to marry this guy," Bruce said. "For Christ's Sake, she must have known something about his character before she married him!"

"Oh, yeah, she did. In fact, she worked for him." Stanley saw the look of astonishment on Bruce's face. "I guess you can really blame me for the marriage. Back then Kate was an executive secretary for the manager of a large garment factory in San Francisco owned by Moroni. Dora, my wife, Kate's mother, became very ill and needed a mastectomy, both breasts." Stanley became quiet for several moments. He continued, "I had finally stopped working for a firm. I had always wanted to go out on my own, have my own plumbing shop, and I had just got started when Dora became ill. I had put off health insurance needing all the bucks we had to get a business going, damn fool that I was. Dora had to go into the hospital and it looked like the welfare route. We couldn't use the doctor we wanted." He paused. "Anyway, Moroni got wind of it, the fact that we needed money real bad. He got a look at Kate, liked what he saw, and then played the big benefactor paying for all the doctor and hospital expense. 'No obligation!' The son-of-a-bitch, no obligation alright! He wanted to bang Kate real bad. She would have none of him that way. He used the bucks he spent and the success of the operation to his advantage and got Kate to feel obligated to him. Finally, she consented to marriage. And that's about it."

"There had to be another way rather than marrying him," Bruce said sadly.

"Hey, believe it or not, a lot of good came out of that marriage," Stanley said. "Dora lived many pain free years after that operation, and I have two wonderful grandchildren. But Kate, John, and Sally are paying the price."

"John?" Bruce questioned.

"A couple of years ago John and Kate started dating," Stanley said. "He was a pharmacist in Longs Drugs at the shopping center. Moroni heard about the relationship and he sent Charlie Dobbs to visit John. Charlie beat him up real bad. John was in the hospital three weeks. He had several broken bones, abrasions, and his hearing was affected. He left this area when the bones healed. He was afraid of being hurt again and I can't blame him for that. He was a nice man."

"What's this Charlie Dobbs to Moroni?" Bruce asked.

"His right hand. Charlie Dobbs does whatever foul job Moroni wants done. I'll bet dollars to doughnuts Charlie placed that arrow in Sally. There was no bow involved. I bet he duct taped her mouth to shut her up. I know this guy, he's a real weasel."

"Placed the arrow!" Bruce said. "My God, it's hard to believe all this."

"Sure! Sally is going to live," Stanley said, "but she'll suffer the consequences of that wound for the rest of her life. That's what Moroni wanted, and Charlie is a professional. That fuckhead, my ex-son-in-law, doesn't give a shit about the dog. But Kate will see the pain in that dog's eyes for the rest of its life, and that's punishment. Kate's punishment for leaving him, and seeing you."

The two men were silent for several moments. "Are you ready to say bye, bye, baby?" Stanley said.

Bruce smiled at the older man. "It's been a few years but I've been around shit before. I wish I was younger though." He paused. "No matter. How old are your grandchildren?"

"Twenty-five."

"Then Kate is forty-nine," Bruce said.

"That's right." Both men looked at each other and started to laugh. "Remember now," Stanley said, "you figured that out all by yourself. I didn't tell you." He looked at his watch. "They have been in there for an hour and seventeen minutes. How long is this thing going to take?"

Kate came into the room with a smile on her face. She went to her father and reached for his hands. "Sally is going to be fine. The arrow has been removed, the wounds cleansed, cauterized, and stitched. She even had a blood transfusion." She saw Bruce and went quickly into his arms hugging him with all her strength. She moved her head and looked into his eyes, and then she looked at his lips. She kissed him. The kiss was light but meaningful. "Thank you, Bruce." She giggled, and then said, "If you hadn't got my head out of my ass I'd still be standing in the backyard."

The veterinarian came into the room and sat on one of the chairs. He, too, looked tired. He said, "Sally will be with us for three or four days but she'll heal. Maybe a touch lame hereafter. Damndest thing I ever saw! If Sally had to be shot, the arrow was in the right place. Another inch to the right and an artery or the heart would have taken it, and that would have been all she wrote. Perfectly aimed, chest area, just to the right of the armpit and exiting behind the right elbow. Nasty, but not life threatening when taken here in time."

31

Bruce and Stanley looked at each other. This time they were not laughing.

Chapter Four

Near Tiller, Oregon.

Bruce and Christy had returned to their home in Oregon. Christy seemed to sniff every inch of their land making sure there were no disturbances. Bruce kept himself busy. He had to keep busy. Otherwise, his thoughts of Kate would control and limit his activity. He decided to think about her only at night. His plan failed.

Their parcel of ground was a little over an acre with an approximate seven hundred foot frontage on the South Umpqua River. About five hundred feet faced the two lane South Umpqua Road which was paved and used primarily by logging trucks and the one hundred and thirty plus people who lived within a radius of five miles. The depth of the property from the road to the river was shallow, about seventy feet on one side and eighty-five feet on the opposite line, and gradually widened making the size of the parcel quite irregular.

At this particular river location, a creek emptied into the river. Boulders were prominent in the water and small waterfalls were numerous. As the waters receded during late spring and summer months fishing holes were obvious and water fowl were seen frequently, and nature's grandeur became softer and gentler.

Their property faced North, the river was on the south side, and the Ackerman's twenty-five foot trailer was permanently placed fifty feet east of Bruce's twenty-nine foot trailer. Tom and Lois Ackerman visited their property and used their trailer three weeks out of every year. The only other neighbor was a small market on the opposite side of the road a block from Bruce's trailer. The market was normally closed during the winter months.

Salmon and trout fishermen plus the deer, elk, duck, and bear hunters continually came. And during the summer season families from Roseburg, Medford, Canyonville, and other

33

communities within a hundred miles, would drive and spend the day at South Umpqua Falls, another fifteen miles northeast of the Ackerman property. The falls were a popular picnic place. And the parents and their children could slide off the flat and slippery boulders into deep pools of water. The environment of river, falls, mountains, and forest was truly beautiful.

Bruce was annoyed with the amount of traffic going by his home. He estimated three hundred vehicles per day which included loggers, hunters, fishermen, and tourists.

"Getting like a damn freeway around here," he mumbled to Christy.

The nights were quiet, and generally autumn, fall, and spring were pleasant, the amount of rainfall being the only concern. Bruce was told that he lived in the 'banana belt' of Oregon having an average annual rainfall of only twenty-eight inches, but during the rainy season he constantly watched the river for signs of flooding.

The riverbank was forty feet below the rear of his trailer pad. The latter was on a twenty-five foot wide by thirty-eight foot long rock foundation that was five foot high in the rear and gradually lessened its height until the concrete surface was level with the driveway in front. As one faced the trailer space from the road there were steps near the left front side going down to a yard with a shed that housed the well and pump.

A satellite dish was also in the yard. There were other concrete steps on the right side of the pad that led to another yard where Bruce's pride and joy were seen, two very large and beautiful silver maple trees, the only ones in the neighborhood. In addition, the property had a wide variety of trees: alder, spruce, fir, pine, the standard maple, oak, aspen, birch. Flowers, most of which were planted by Bruce, were abundant. And the grass and shrubbery in both yards were nourished and manicured.

The trailer faced the driveway and George with the road just beyond. From every window in the trailer there was a pretty view of the river, creek, trees, mountains, or yard. Behind the foundation, and just before the ground sloped severely to the riverbank, was an eight by twelve foot storage shed, old but watertight. All garden tools, trailer accessories, and storage boxes were kept there. Bruce had a garden hose attached to the trailer from the well. He had 30amp electric, a phone, and the rig was connected to one of the property's two septic tanks. Refuse, any amount and all kinds, was free and hauled by George to a refuse deposit located between Tiller and the property.

Bruce knew the rent was very reasonable but he had worked hard to make this place even more beautiful, and the river view more spectacular. Over fifty Suburban loads of foliage, weeds, small to medium trees, and overhanging tree branches were hauled to the refuse area. The owners were delighted with the results and Bruce was pleased. He was pleased not only with the views and landscaping but with the knowledge that he could still accomplish physical labor after bypass surgery. The job took time and he worked slowly and rested frequently. For the first time, he was aware that he had to work differently than before surgery.

Five days had elapsed since their return from Sonoma. They had been gone long enough for the yards to begin looking shabby. Bruce cut the grass, removed weeds and saplings, and leaves were raked. He watered the yards and plants, swept and washed down the trailer pad, and trimmed the two pathways to the riverbank, one on each end of the property. His current project was the cleaning of the Suburban and trailer, inside and out. Tomorrow, he and Christy would drive into Canyonville, twenty-eight miles southwest, do his laundry, and replenish groceries and meats.

The dinner dishes were washed and he watched the news on television although he did not hear the commentator. His thoughts were of Kate. He decided to phone her. He sat on the edge of the double bed near the phone on the small nightstand. He would ask about Sally but his real purpose was to tell her that he needed her. He felt that she would become reticent and

35

defensive when she heard what he wanted. He probably would lose her but he decided that a platonic relationship was not what he wanted.

He dialed. He was very nervous.

"Hello," Kate said.

"Kate?" Bruce said.

"Yes." She paused. "Is that you, Bruce?"

"Yes."

"I'm so glad. I miss you so. I think of you all the time. I just can't help myself," she said.

"Oh, Kate, I miss you, too." He was relieved and his words came rapidly. "I need to see you. I need to be with you. I need to love you. I want to hold you. I, just need to be with you. We can't skirt the truth anymore. We either are, or we aren't."

He paused, very aware of no response. "I think I love you. I want us to love each other, to learn to love each other, to really know one another. If it's just me with these thoughts, tell me now so I can get on with my life and to try and forget you. Quite frankly, to try and forget that I want you so." He was rambling but he was sincere. "There must be truth between us, no evasiveness. Each must know what the other feels. I'm going to stop talking. I must know now what you really think and feel."

"I think and feel the same way you do, Bruce. I want to hold you, and be with you, to really know you, and to love you in every way," she said softly.

"My God, that's what I wanted to hear," he said. And he felt grateful that another woman could love him.

"But I'm so afraid, Bruce."

"We can't be in fear of what someone else might do. We have to live our lives truthfully, and express our feelings, to the world if we wish to. If we are unable to do this, then there's no point in living. And I'm not referring just to us, but anyone in our predicament. Evil must never rule a person's life."

"Get off your soapbox, Bruce, I'm talking about your life! To put it more bluntly, your death!" She started to cry. "Dad told me of your conversation, about my ex-husband." She paused for several moments. "Oh, Bruce, I want to love you, but I don't want you to die! Oh my, this is all so terrible!"

"Not the way we feel about one another." He could hear her crying harder, and he waited for her sobs to subside. "Let me worry about Moroni wanting to hurt me," he said. "Believe in me. And should I fail, we would have loved, and that's all that really matters. We're not running away from this son-of-a-bitch, or from each other! Not now!"

"Goddamn it! You're not listening! You're not impregnable! And you're over sixty years old!" She hung up.

He sat on the side of the bed for a longtime. He thought about calling her back but there was nothing more to say. He hoped she would call him back but he felt she wouldn't. He thought of her loveliness, his wanting to know her better, and he knew that he would never stop thinking about her.

Glenn Mathews

Chapter Five

Bruce sat on a boulder in the shade by the river. His hair was disheveled and he had not shaved for three days and the gray stubble was not becoming. He was grateful for the shade. The weather was hot. The weather always seemed hot to him around Labor Day, just three days hence. The river looked cool, gentle, and inviting. He threw a tennis ball in the river for Christy. The dog raced into the water and grabbed the ball in her mouth at mid-stream. She paddled down the river going with the mild current until there were no ripples. She then headed for shore about fifty yards from where her master sat. She was dripping wet but waited until she was quite close to Bruce before she vigorously shook herself.

She pranced near Bruce until she dropped the ball several feet in front of him. Bruce stood and went to the ball and threw it again in the river. Christy jumped into the water, her head high, her tail acting like a paddle, and she went immediately for the little yellow blob on the water.

Bruce watched her but he was thinking about Kate. A week had elapsed since their phone conversation. He knew he would call her again but had postponed doing so believing the results would prove conclusive. He felt their relationship had ended but he did not really want to know that it had.

"Hey, down there, do you need another playmate?" Kate yelled. She stood at the top edge of the yard. She laughed.

Bruce turned and saw her. He went to the pathway and climbed the hill as quickly as he could. They stood a few feet apart and they just looked at each other. They smiled. Her white short sleeve blouse showed a hint of cleavage under a gold necklace. The brown slacks were trim but not tight. She wore a small simple watch on her left wrist and white flats and socks on her feet. He wore faded blue denim trousers, a dirty yellow and blue plaid short sleeve shirt, dirty white tennis shoes and brown socks.

She laughed. "You do dress conservatively. And your shirt is dirty, and you need a shave."

"I don't care." He grinned.

They walked into each other's arms and embraced tightly. Neither said a word. He looked at her and examined her hair, the eyebrows, the eyes, nose, and mouth. There were tears in her eyes. He blew gently on the full wavy hair over her brow. They kissed for a longtime. There was no searching with tongues, or pressing hard with their mouths. They kissed and enjoyed their nearness.

Their mouths separated and they continued to embrace.

"I thought I lost you," he said.

"Never," she said.

Christy came alongside them and shook her coat, the spray went over them.

"She has to make her presence known." Bruce laughed.

Kate knelt on the ground and hugged the wet dog. "I've missed you, Christy. And, I've brought a friend!"

"Did you bring Sally?" Bruce said. He took Kate's hand and they walked eagerly toward the front of the property.

"Yes, I did. I couldn't leave her home knowing there was a river where I was going, not to mention you and Christy."

"When I phoned I meant to ask how she was," Bruce said, "but I guess you and I were -- uppermost. Well, I guess --"

"I know." She squeezed his hand. "She's fine. A little stiff and lame in that leg, but the stitches are out, and she'll get better with the lameness, I'm sure."

They had reached the car and Kate opened the door on the passenger side. Bruce slid in and Sally jumped from the rear to the front seat. Bruce gave her a hug and the white dog slopped his cheeks and chin with her tongue.

"Put that leash on her." Kate pointed to the floorboard by his feet. "She'll always have to be tied up or on a leash when she's outside here. Otherwise, she'd head for the water and then God knows where!"

Glenn Mathews

Bruce snapped the leash on the dog and brought her outside the car. Christy and Sally immediately renewed acquaintance. Tails wagged and Christy excitedly whined her welcome and approval. The four of them walked toward the river. When they reached the pathway to the riverbank Bruce took the leash off Sally. The two dogs took off and were immediately in the water. A big grin was on Sally's face.

"Oh, Bruce, it might be too soon for Sally to swim," Kate said.

"It's nearly a hundred degrees out here, she's about as healed as she's going to be, and the exercise and water will do her good," Bruce smiled. "Look at them! They're almost as happy as I am!" He took her into his arms and he kissed her.

They walked down the pathway to the river jabbering and laughing like two small children.

Kate's suitcase and overnight case were brought into the trailer and Bruce arranged space next to his clothes in the larger closet, and there was one empty drawer below the closet. He turned the air conditioner higher, and he quickly removed his articles on the lower shelf of the medicine cabinet. He was thankful that he had thoroughly cleaned the trailer the day before.

Kate put her clothes in the closet. "What is the dog basket doing on your bed?" she said.

"I put it there during waking hours and then at bedtime it goes on the living room floor between the couch and TV," Bruce said. "I'm going to place Sally's bed pillow on top of Christy's basket on the bed and later I'll put it in front of the kitchen door. Then I'll put the occasional chair on top of the sofa so her pillow will fit better, and then she'll be next to Christy."

"You got it all figured out. Don't you?" She smiled.

"I try."

"There's just one thing."

"What's that?" he questioned.

"What if I sleep on the sofa?" Kate said.

His face got quite red. He looked at her and saw the serious expression unaware of being teased. "Well, I guess, that's right. I'll find another place for the chair. But I'll sleep on the sofa."

She didn't have to move far to put her arms around him. "I didn't come here to sleep on the sofa, silly," she murmured.

"I'm glad," he said softly. He knew she wanted to go to bed with him now but he didn't know how to get her there. He felt awkward, wanting to postpone their lovemaking. Sure, he thought, I could kiss her hard, fumble for brassiere and panties, push her on the bed and enter her. But he wanted their love to be special. He worried that he may not get an erection. Many years had passed since he had sex with a woman and then he had failed as a lover. He didn't want to fail again.

He went to the freezer and removed an ice tray, took a bottle of white wine from the refrigerator, and got two wine glasses from the cupboard. "How about wine and special views from my patio?"

"Sounds wonderful," Kate said.

Bruce had placed two patio chairs, one lounge chair, two side tables and a grass textured outdoor carpet under the trailer awning. To the rear of the trailer pad and next to this patio was an old bathtub that was recessed, its top level with the concrete surface. The tub was filled with dirt and Bruce had planted dahlias, petunias, and snapdragons. All the flowers were blooming.

They sat on the patio and enjoyed the scenery. Christy lay untethered next to her master. Sally was next to Kate but a small rope was attached to her collar and then fastened to the rear bumper of the trailer. Several minutes elapsed as they sipped their wine. "I can understand why you live here," Kate said. "So much beauty and everything is so peaceful." She pointed to the bird feeders. "Look, Bruce, the blue jays use that one on the tree but the little guys use the one on the stump."

"That's right," he said. "The jays always feed from that one until a big mockingbird comes along and then they scatter. The mockingbird is boss and he gets the feeder all to himself, but

41

Glenn Mathews

never seems to bother the sparrows or the little birds at the other feeder. He has his own code of ethics, I guess."

"I like it here so much," she said. "I don't think there can be a place anywhere as beautiful as this."

"I know." Bruce paused a moment. "How long can you stay?"

"One week, including the traveling time. The drive takes me about seven hours from Sonoma. Can you put up with me for that long?"

"Yes, and maybe even longer!" He grinned. "Who's working the gift shop for you?"

"Two ladies, friends, who like to work part-time once in awhile. They'll alternate with Debra who'll work full-time in my absence."

"How did you find me?"

"Well, you'd told me where Tiller was and I finally did find it on the map. When I arrived there I went to the little post office and asked the postmistress if she knew where you lived. She told me to go exactly five miles on South Umpqua Road and your nameplate was on the right. I had the feeling she had a crush on you. She's a good-looking woman!"

"And very happily married I may add. Diana has become a friend." He reached for her hand. "Now, while you are here you stay out of my kitchen. I do all the cooking. I may let you wipe a few dishes. There's lots of places I want to take you. We'll drive out to the falls. I'll take you to see the tallest sugar pine tree. Tallest in the world and just eleven miles from here, I'll have you know."

Bruce rattled, excited, and he wanted her to see all the places that meant something to him. "We'll drive over to Shady Cove and have dinner. There's a very nice place to dine right by the Rogue River. And I want to take you to Jacksonville, west of Medford. The inn there is supposedly the best place to eat in Oregon. I want to take you to Ashland, a pleasant town and very well known for their legitimate theaters. We'll take in a matinee one day. And --"

42

"Hold on! Whoa! When do we sleep?" Kate interrupted.

He looked at her and kissed her hand.

"I'm sure we will find lots of time to sleep," he said quietly.

They had finished dinner and the dishes. Bruce turned on the television. There would be a movie on soon and he wanted to show off the great reception he got through the satellite system. He decided to sit by Kate on the sofa.

"I really like your trailer, Bruce," she said. "But why did you decide on a kitchen in front?"

"Oh, I don't know. When a kitchen is in the middle of the rig it's usually next to the bathroom."

He was very aware of her nearness. He knew that she had recently put perfume on and she smelled wonderful. "And I like the bathroom next to the bedroom, between the bedroom and the living room."

"I see." She took a throw pillow and placed it on Bruce's lap. She lay on her side with her head on the pillow and faced the television.

"Besides, you don't get a lot of traffic walking through on you with the kitchen in front." He felt the fullness of her left breast on his thigh.

"Do you get many visitors?" she said.

"No."

"Oh. I'm glad you shaved," she said.

"Yes, I feel cleaner," he said.

"Beautiful television reception." She lightly placed her hand on his leg just below the knee.

"Yes, and all kinds of stations. I can order just what I want," he said. "I've got the cable channels, all kinds of sports. I really enjoy the Atlanta Braves and I get them live six times a week unless they're traveling and that's only a day once in awhile. Imagine that! Way out here in the boondocks!" He felt like a virgin.

"How wonderful." She took his right hand and placed it on her right breast.

He gently massaged her breast.

"I like that," she murmured.

He began to relax. He wanted very much to see her breasts. He unbuttoned the blouse. She sat and took off the blouse. He searched for the snaps to the brassiere.

"In front," she said quietly.

He unsnapped the brassiere and she removed it. From behind, he placed a hand on each of her breasts. "They're very lovely," he whispered.

"Just for you," she said.

He softly kissed the back of her neck many times as he caressed her breasts. She stood and took off her slacks. She wore black hosiery, a garter belt, and no panties.

"You did more than just put on perfume," he said.

"Yes. I want to excite you. I want you to want me."

"I want you very much." He felt the beginnings of an erection. He examined the cheeks of her buttocks and thought they were perfect. He placed his hands on her rump and turned her. His face was level with her pubic patch, and he began rubbing his nose and mouth between her legs, and he kissed the inside of her thighs above the hosiery. His hands lingered over her legs enjoying their erotic silkiness. He was quite hard now. He took her hands and pulled her towards him, to his lap. She came into his arms and they kissed. Their mouths opened wider, lips kissing and exploring. Their tongues touched. He sucked her tongue into his mouth and he began to squeeze her left breast.

She moaned, "Take me to bed, Bruce. I want you in me. Oh, God, how I want you in me!"

He stood, took her hand and led her to the bedroom.

They saw the dog beds, and they began to laugh.

"Where are they?" She was laughing hard now.

He looked back, beyond the living room. "I think Christy is under the dinette table. Sally's in front of her laying on the floor between the table and the kitchen sink with her back toward me."

He sat on the sofa laughing uncontrollably. "And I've lost my erection."

"Not for long. But get these beds down." She was becoming hysterical. "I had a hunch these beds were going to play their part."

He put the chair on the sofa, Sally's bed by the front door, and Christy's basket next to it. "There, just like I said."

Both howled with laughter.

He went toward the bed and his laughter became less, and ceased. He saw her on the bed. He saw the complete nudity, the black enticements, and he began to stare. He became hard quickly. Her laughter became giggles and then she saw his look and she became quiet. His erection was very evident under the fabric. She lay back on the bed, her legs dangled over the side. She spread her legs wide inviting him to love her there. He kneeled on the floor between her thighs and placed his arms under the satiny legs, his hands clutching the cheeks of her buttocks. His mouth was on her vulva, his tongue sought the clitoris. He licked. He kissed. He sucked. He removed his pants and shorts, continuing to love her at the same time. He stood. A vein on his penis was quite prominent and he was large. "Look at me," he said. "I've never felt so large. I feel wonderful!"

She looked. "You are wonderful. Put it in my mouth!"

He quickly removed his shirt and went on the bed. His legs straddled her upper right arm. He leaned forward and she placed the penis in her mouth, sucking and mouthing him for several minutes. He almost came, but he waited. She licked and kissed his shaft and gently licked and kissed his testicles.

"I can't wait any longer. I've got to get inside you," he said.

"I want you inside me. Now." She pushed her entire body onto the bed.

He went on his knees between her legs and forced her thighs wider apart. He entered her. She was very wet and he had the most marvelous feelings as he went back and forth, back and forth, endlessly. He penetrated her as far as he could and then deliberately he almost came out of her, teasing, gently probing

45

Glenn Mathews

her. Abruptly, he penetrated her deeply and then repeated the rhythmic back and forth motion.

"Don't stop! Please don't stop! It's wonderful!" She kissed him and tongued him all over his face and ears. "Let me get on top of you!" she screamed.

He lay on his back and she straddled him, quickly placing the penis inside her. "Let me do it!" she demanded. "Just lay still!"

She moved on him, up and down. Gradually, her movements quickened. She stopped and lay on top of him, her legs between his, her upper thigh gently squeezing his testicles. Slowly, her pelvic area began to move, to rock back and forth, and sideways. His penis was deep inside her. "Suck my tongue," she said quickly.

He sucked, his arms embraced her tightly. She withdrew her tongue. "Oh, my goodness," she whispered. "My goodness. How marvelous."

"What is?" he said.

"Didn't you feel it?" she said.

"Feel what?"

"The pressure, the contractions, my vagina squeezing your penis," she said quietly. "It's so wonderful. I feel so completely empty and relaxed. I've had an orgasm! I never had one before."

"An orgasm?" He couldn't believe it. He had felt the pressure, and the squeezing. He had never before experienced a woman having an orgasm. He knew they had them but he never knew what they were like. He was very pleased with himself. He felt like a man. "What is it like for you?" he said.

She did not answer for a few moments. "Like reaching the top of a waterfall and then sliding over. A completeness. A wonderful emptiness when once you were so full. Anyway, it's hard to explain."

They pushed the spread back and got under the sheets. He took her into his arms and he kissed her forehead.

"I had a really good time," she said sleepily. "I hope you had a really good time."

"I had a very really good time," he said.

"I'm sorry you didn't come."

"I'm not," he said. "The fun would have ended sooner. Besides, I'll have lots of opportunity. Won't we?"

He glanced down. She was sound asleep.

Like young lovers they held hands wherever they went. He took her to see the matinee of Richard III in Ashland, Oregon. Afterwards, they walked the downtown portion and went into an old-fashioned ice cream parlor and had chocolate sodas. On their way home they had dinner at Bel-Dis, a restaurant by the Rogue River in Shady Cove. Bruce had made arrangements for a special window table and they enjoyed watching rafts on the river, Canadian geese, and the mallards.

"What does Bel-Dis mean?" he said to the waitress.

"I think it has something to do with an aria from the opera Madame Butterfly," she said. "But I can find out for sure."

Kate smiled. "That's not necessary. This is such a nice place. We just wanted to know what the name meant." She reached across the table for Bruce's hand. "I want to come back here again, darling."

They took a picnic and went to South Umpqua Falls, and although they did not swim, the dogs did.

They went to the Jacksonville Inn and had dinner, and agreed that the food and service were excellent. They walked the streets of the historical little village and went into one of its shops. Bruce bought Kate a small sprinkling can, an ornament filled with colorful artificial flowers.

"When I get home to Sonoma I'll put this in the living room, and sometimes I'll use real flowers in it," she said. "It will always remind me of my trip to Tiller, but especially of, of all the things we did together."

He took her to the tallest sugar pine tree in a very remote area.

"Listen," she said. "To the stillness, all around us. I feel so close to, I don't know. Is it God? But I'm not very religious." She hunched her shoulders. "Anyway, I talked to this beautiful tree, and the tree said to enjoy ourselves and to be together." She kissed him.

"You talked to this tree?" he said.

"Yes. I talk to all kinds of things. I talk to plants, trees, flowers, animals. We enjoy each other."

His eyes were wide open. "And they talk back to you?"

"Yes."

"What do you talk about?"

"I ask them if they are doing well, and if they are happy, and if there is anything I can do to help them," Kate said. "And they're just as considerate of me."

"Kate, this is all very nice and cute, but very childish. You can't talk to these kinds of things, sweetheart."

"But I do, darling. It's not childish. Simple, maybe. You talk to Christy all the time, and I'm sure she answers you." She kissed the tip of his nose, turned and walked toward the car.

He smiled as he watched her go. He wasn't about to argue with her. Yesterday morning she was in the yard while he straightened up the trailer. He looked out the window and she was near the bird feeder where the sparrows came. She was within three feet of that feeder and there were more birds there than he had ever seen. And he thought at the time that she was talking to them.

Chapter Six

The living room was very large. Its fireplace was enormous. The bookcases were voluminous. The furniture was expensive, bulky, but not intimate or inviting, and the carpeting was lavish but not appropriate.

The big wing chair overwhelmed Karen Moroni. She was petite, mid-twenties, blue eyes, light brown hair that cascaded around her ears and just touched her shoulders highlighting her chiseled features. She had a hint of lipstick on sensuous lips, a characteristic of her mother's, and her bust was small but rewarding. She wore a cream colored suit with knee length skirt, a dark blue long sleeved blouse and mid-heel shoes, its blue matching the blouse. The hosiery on her shapely legs complemented the suit. "What a God awful room!" she said. "Makes you wonder where the caskets are. Far cry from when Mom lived here. I don't like this place. Eddie, why the hell are we here?"

"We've gone all through that, Karen. We've got to talk to the old fart. He's doing some terrible things to Mom and he's got to stop!" The young man who spoke was the young lady's brother, and her twin. He, too, was small in stature. He was not particularly handsome, but he had a manly quality. He had a full head of brown hair, not parted, hazel eyes, and a rounded face that was wholesome looking and always seemed attentive. According to the charts, his weight was perfect. He wore a simple brown suit, a pale yellow dress shirt, and a brown tie with a Windsor knot.

Roy, the Filipino servant, came into the room.

"Your father has just returned from Mass," he said. "He's taking a moment to change and to freshen up. He will be with you soon." The big man left the room.

"Freshen up, alright, I bet the maid is giving him a blow job," Karen said.

Eddie laughed. "Probably, wheelchair and all. I can just picture it. But I'll bet the maid's a looker!"

49

"You're terrible, Eddie! It makes no difference if she's a looker. The results are the same."

They laughed. "We sure had to keep our sense of humor around this joint," he said. "At least, until we got out of here and went to college. But you still have a dirty mind. Very risque, indeed!"

"I inherited that characteristic from my brother." She listened. "Hark! Do I hear movement yonder? The mortician may be arriving."

Vincent Moroni entered the room. He looked frail, but clean. He had poor posture in his chair. His head was held slightly lower than normal, and his back showed the beginnings of a hunchback. He wore a black robe with a gold design over gold silk pajamas. Black slippers and socks were on his feet. The wheelchair he sat on was pushed by the maid.

The maid wore a black dress with white collar and cuff. The hemline was well above her knee. She wore high heeled shoes and black hosiery. She was in her early twenties and she was very curvaceous.

The twins gave each other a knowing look.

"Get out of here," Moroni said bluntly to the maid. "And close the doors when you leave." His voice was strong, but his body smelled of age.

The large double doors closed.

"Well, now, how nice to see my children again. I had forgotten what you look like."

"How have you been, Father?" Eddie said.

"In pain, but surviving," Moroni said.

"Are you getting around better?" Karen said.

Neither child kissed or embraced him.

"Do you really care?" Moroni said. "Let's cut out this palaver. What is it you really want? What do you need? Money? Are you in trouble?" He glared at them.

"Nice to know that we've been missed," Eddie said sarcastically. "We don't need your help, Father. You're the one that needs help!"

"Listen, sonny boy, we all need help," Moroni said. "Yes, even I need help! How do you think I got the use of my right leg back? Huh? And my left leg, I'm just beginning to get some feeling out of it." Moroni spit when he talked angrily, and saliva was on his chin. He took a handkerchief out of the pocket of his robe and wiped his face. "God helped me, that's who! Every Sunday I go to church and it's paying off." He began to whine pathetically. "I plead to Him. I beseech Him. I tell Him to please give me back my strength and the use of my legs. And He is doing it! I keep my end of the bargain, too, and I help the church."

"How many thousands of dollars have you given the cardinal, Father? And I do mean the cardinal. Does he wash away all your sins, too?" Karen spoke quietly. She was angry but unlike her brother, she kept her calm.

The old man looked at his daughter disgustedly. "You don't really know. Really know! The pain I've suffered. And not just physical pain. I loved your mother. Do you hear me? I loved your mother! When she left me I had a terrible stroke. She caused that! Thank God only my legs were involved." He looked at the ceiling. "Oh, God," he whined. "Thank you, thank you!"

"Yes, thank God, you sure as hell wouldn't want to give up banging some broad, or whatever," Karen said.

He glanced at her, his dark sunken eyes hateful. "You have a foul mouth, daughter. If you weren't my flesh and blood, I'd--"

"Kill me, Father?"

"Thrash you within an inch of your life!"

"When I was a teenager you did that once. Or, had it done. Remember, Daddy?"

Eddie stood between the old man and his sister. "You've got to blame somebody. Don't you? Any problem, it's somebody else's fault. You never take the blame for your own foolishness or for the way you live. Mother didn't cause your stroke. You did. Ask a doctor. You know what causes a stroke? Smoking, drinking, drugs, pressure, and add whoring. You've had it all to excess, but I bet you just keep doing it." He went to the wheelchair and looked down on his father. The old man averted his eyes. "And now this religious shit. Why? You afraid the great Vincent Moroni, godfather to shit and evil, is going to croak? Are you paving the way? You never went to church when we were growing up. Same old shit. You're nothing but an evil hypocrite."

Moroni breathed heavily. He raised his head and stared at his son. He pressed his lips together. Anger and hate consumed him.

Eddie saw the look. "Yeah, I know, if I weren't your son, you'd have me killed." He sat on a large sofa and crossed his legs.

"You two have shown me nothing but disrespect," Moroni said. "All your lives!" He wiped his mouth. He spoke quietly. "And I am respected and loved by many people in this country, some I don't even know exist. And my own children. Yes, my own children who I show love, affection and kindness to --"

"Love and kindness? You got to be kidding." Eddie shook his head. "No, you don't kid. What love and kindness?"

"You are doing very well for the brokerage firm in San Francisco. Aren't you?" Moroni displayed an ugly smile and a self-satisfied expression on his face. He spoke slowly. "Twenty-five years old and already they are offering you a junior partnership. I wonder why? Could it be that you have attracted several million dollar accounts? I wonder where those accounts came from?" The whine had returned in his voice and his expression was now one of innocence.

Eddie looked at his father for several moments. He nodded his head. "Yes, I know where the money and clients came from. Family money. From those people that respect you so much."

"I sent money, too, under another name."

"I know that," Eddie said. "I should have come here much sooner and thanked you. You deserved a thank you because in your own way you tried to help me. You wanted your son to get ahead in life and for that I am grateful." He got up from the sofa and sat on its arm, looking at his father. "But if I had come to see you I would have asked you to remove your money from my firm, and to ask your friends to do so. I don't want to work with those kind of people and that kind of money. Believe me, I am no do-gooder, but all that money has a history of misery."

"I give the people what they want! And money is money! You're a damn fool to think like that!" his father shouted.

"Maybe. There are many that would agree with you," Eddie said. "All the senior partners would agree with you. I don't deserve being a junior partner. There's much I don't know in the stock market and other investment fields. And I don't like the profession. That's why I quit two days ago." He sat on the sofa again.

"Quit? Quit! You can't just quit when you have a career at stake. You're making big money and you will be making more!" Moroni looked at his son. He kept looking at him. He shook his head. He waved his right hand at Eddie. "I wash my hands of you."

"Thank you, I appreciate that," Eddie said.

"And what is the great thinker going to do now?" Moroni said caustically.

"Go back to school and be a doctor. I have been accepted at the UCLA School of Medicine. I start next month."

"And what are you going to use for money? There's four years of schooling ahead of you, if you make it."

"I saved some, and there's my trust fund. That money can't be used for any better purpose," Eddie said.

"Yes, your trust fund. My money. My help again." Moroni smiled. The smile became an evil grin. "Strange, but how can my trust fund money be so clean?"

"You have a point," Eddie said. "But, maybe, I can bring some good out of it. And Mom had something to do with that money. You were married many years. As I recall, Mom kept after you to establish trust funds for Karen and me. You finally gave in."

53

"Your mother didn't make any money. I made the money. She just took care of you kids and the household. I make the money," the old man insisted.

"She lived with you for over twenty years. And took care of you, too," Karen blurted. "She gave this household some real respectability. And that's worth considerable!"

Moroni wheeled himself closer to his daughter's chair and glared at her. "And what are you going to do with your trust fund? Spend it on that ugly big lanky Kraut?"

Karen wasn't surprised by his remark. "I figured you knew about him," she said. "What else do you know about us?"

"Let's see now, I have to think back, but I still have a very good memory," her father said. "You live in a suburb of Chicago, a rental, and you work for a drug or pharmaceutical firm. You're secretary to a big shot, type well, take shorthand, and know the computer. You earn about thirty-two thousand dollars a year, plus bonus. Not bad for a woman, especially at your age. They like you and you have a pretty good future with them."

Karen started to open her mouth.

"Don't interrupt me!" Moroni said. "Now, about your boyfriend. You haven't shacked up with him, yet. He's a year older than you, has never been married, and he works for the same firm. He makes a good salary, executive caliber, and he knows his field in computer engineering, or some such stuff. I've been told he looks like hell." He stopped talking. There was no response. "You can say something now," he said.

"You're very good. My goodness, your underworld subordinates do their jobs well," she exclaimed. "But, please, let me fill you in for a complete picture." Karen paused. "I love this Kraut. Yes, he's German, and he's very tall, and thin. He already is well respected in his field, having a brilliant mind. He may not be very handsome, but he loves me, and he's kind to me. He is thoughtful and considerate. I am going to add some of my trust fund money to his savings and we're going to make a nice down payment on a house after we're married. Then, I will use the rest of my trust fund to help me get my teacher's credentials. I want to teach. Richard and I plan to marry next year." Karen uncrossed her legs and moved slightly forward in her chair. "I want to make something very clear. Don't ever, ever try to hurt him or anyone close to me because you want to get back at me for some warped reason. If you do, I'll make life hell on earth for you! I'm not afraid of you, and I know a great deal about you! Don't ever do to me what you are doing to Mother!" She was very angry now.

"Don't you threaten me!" The old man was almost falling out of his chair. "No one threatens me! You could be no problem, believe me!" He sat back in his chair, breathing hard, and he wiped his chin again.

There was silence.

"What is this business about your mother," he said.

"That's why we came here, to ask that you leave her alone," Eddie said.

"Leave her alone? Leave who alone?" the old man said. "If you mean your mother, I haven't seen her in over four years."

"We know that, but you arranged for things to happen," Eddie said. "A couple of years ago Mom's business was ransacked and much of the inventory was broken. A friend, a man that she liked, was beaten brutally by Charlie. And recently her dog was almost killed. All because she was seeing another man. Mother doesn't know that we came here and --"

"How do you know it was Charlie?" Moroni interrupted.

"He told Mom what his assailant looked like. It was Charlie," Eddie replied.

"Then he should have gone to the police," the old man said.

"He was afraid to. When he could, he left town. He was very frightened," Karen said calmly.

He looked at each of them hatefully. He spoke slowly and quietly. "You come here to my house and accuse me of doing certain things that you have no proof of. You have no right to do that. You have insulted me. You have shown me disrespect. You have lied about me, and you have threatened me." Loudly,

"Get out of my house! I want nothing further to do with either of you!"

"We'll go," Eddie started to rise. ""But please leave Mother alone now. She has a right to enjoy life. Let her be!"

"Get out," Moroni said.

"Please leave Mom alone. Don't hurt those that are close to her," Karen said. "She means nothing to you now. And I'm sure that you see other women, and that's fine with all of us."

"Shut up! Don't ever tell me what I can and can't do." A sadistic smile appeared on the old face. "Do you want to know something? I will disinherit you both! You've never been my children. You have always been her fawning brats. Get out of my house! Now!" Again, he wiped his chin.

The children stood and went toward the doors. Eddie stopped. Karen waited. "I'm very happy to hear that we are not getting your money or property," Eddie said quietly. "And I know that I can speak for Karen, too." He smiled at the old man. There was sadness in the smile. "Who are you leaving it all to? Charlie? Roy? Members of your other family? And, don't forget the maid, she's got to be worth bucks. By the way, do you still take penicillin?" He took his sister's hand and they left the house.

They got to the car.

"We probably made matters worse," Karen said.

"I guess, but I hope not. I sure hope not. We tried."

Karen tried to cheer him up. "You liked the maid. Didn't you?"

He smiled at his sister. "Yeah, I bet she'd be something."

"When the lights go out, what difference does it make what we look like?" Karen said.

"Then, sis, why do you keep going to the hairdresser?"

They laughed. Eddie started the car. He drove down the driveway to the outer road for the last time.

The old man sat in his chair. He was upset. He wheeled himself to the liquor cabinet, got a tall glass, filled it half full of

56

bourbon, and added a small amount of soda. He flipped up the flat piece of wood that was under his armrest and he set his drink on it. He removed a half pack of Camels and a book of matches from the pocket of his robe. He lit the cigarette and inhaled deeply, exhaling the majority of smoke through his nose. He drank half his highball.

"She has a right to enjoy life!" he thought aloud. "What about me? The pain I've suffered because of that woman. The pain I'm suffering! She's controlled their minds, that's what she's done. She was always in control of them, and they were all against me no matter what I did for them. And they had it all. Whatever they wanted, I gave them. And what do I get in return? They humiliate me, that's what. Threats. Insults. Disrespect. Imagine me, disrespect."

In a large crystal ashtray on the coffee table, he put out his cigarette. He wheeled slowly to a wall and pressed the buzzer. The maid arrived. "Get me Charlie," he said. "And, you, don't go anywhere. I want you around tonight."

"Yes, Mister Moroni." She left.

Charlie entered the room. He wore dark brown slacks and a tan turtleneck. Moroni handed him his empty glass.

"Get me a drink." He took two swallows when he received the refill.

"Are they still in Oregon?" he said.

"No, Mister Moroni, your ex is in Sonoma. Smitty just got back. He's in his room over the garage."

"Get him."

Charlie left and returned in four minutes. Smitty was short, obese, heavily jowled, balding, mid-thirties, wore glasses and a mustache, and he was very strong. "I just got back, Mister Moroni," Smitty said. "And I was about to come and give you my report but --"

"Give it to me now. What did they do in Oregon?"

"Sir, do you want to know all the details?"

"All the details, Smitty. Everything."

"Well, sir, they went to places of interest in the area, and they went out to eat a couple of times." Smitty paused a moment. "And they did a lot of fucking, Mister Moroni."

"How do you know that, Smitty?" the old man said quietly.

"Well, Mister Moroni, sir," Smitty said, "I couldn't get too close to his trailer because of the dogs hearing me, but I was close enough to hear their sounds and some talk. Like, 'suck me', that was said several times, and 'put it in me'. And twice I heard her scream. You know, Mister Moroni, like she was coming and having an orgasm." Smitty looked at Charlie to see if he had any criticism of him on his face. There was none. "You know, he lives out in the boonies and they thought no one would hear them, or see them."

"See them?" Moroni sipped his drink.

"Well, sir, one night about ten o'clock the moon was out big and bright. It lit up the river like a Christmas tree. You didn't need the yard light to see. He switched that off and put a blanket down on the grass overlooking the river. They took off their robes and lay down. Naked they were, and they sixty-nined it. Whew-eee, that was something to see! Eh, do you know what I mean by sixty-nineing it, Mister Moroni?"

"I'm familiar with the term. Go ahead."

"Well, sir, they could sure teach a few tricks. I saw a movie once where this gal places a big cock in her mouth all the way to the hilt, and this gal, eh, the ex-Mrs. Moroni, did the same thing. And suck? Goll-yyy! And this guy was on her cunt, eh, the opening to her hole. Licking her like an ice cream cone, and sucking her until she moaned and screamed in--, real pleasure. What a sight! Whew-eee!"

"Thank you, Smitty, you did a good job." Moroni spoke quietly. "Now listen to me, Smitty, and listen good. Go back to your room and relax, but never repeat what you just told me. Clear it out of your mind for good. You are to forget what you saw in Oregon. You are to forget that you were in Oregon. Never speak about this again, to anyone. Do you understand? Do you have any questions? Ask them now because if you disobey you know what will happen to you. Wherever you are, you know what will happen to you."

"No, sir, Mister Moroni, I have no questions, and I understand completely," Smitty said. "My mouth is shut on--, what we discussed here tonight. It stays shut!"

"Good. In the morning Charlie will have an envelope for you. You will be pleased with its contents. You can leave now."

"Yes, sir. Thank you, Mister Moroni." Smitty left the room.

The old man stared at nothing. Silence prevailed for several minutes.

Charlie found a chair close by and sat.

Moroni made his plan. He became aware of Charlie. "What is the name of the man from Oregon?"

"Bruce Campbell."

"When Bruce Campbell returns to Sonoma, and he will return to Sonoma soon, I want him hurt-, bad." Moroni became pensive again. Then, he said, "It is not necessary that he should die, but I want it worse than the other one. Should he die, that would be unfortunate. Have it done near her home so she will see him. It must be done quietly. No one must see it done. Keep an eye on her place. There will be no long wait. They will want to fuck. Oh, and have her gift shop vandalized again. After the beating."

"Mister Moroni," Charlie said. "You've been saying 'having it done'. Don't you want me to take care of this?"

"No, you've been in Sonoma before. Send someone who's never been there and who is very good at what he does." Moroni smiled. "No, don't just send someone, send Roy. I understand he is a black belt. The results will be very interesting."

Charlie left. The old man was alone with his thoughts. "They ridicule me," he mumbled. "They insult me. She taught them to show disrespect. She poisoned their minds. A woman most foul raised my children. A lustful carnal woman who left the embrace of my care. She will learn now." He began to whine. "It is too late. I can not forgive. She must be punished. And they wonder where my money will go?" He looked at the

Glenn Mathews

ceiling. "Oh, God," he said loudly. "You will receive the fruits of my labors. You understand me. You forgive me. You heal me. And You are my only companion."

Chapter Seven

October, 1991.

Bay Meadows Race Track is located in San Mateo, California. San Mateo is on the same peninsula as San Francisco and is one of many attractive southern communities. The racetrack, completed in the mid-thirties, was deliberately built adjacent to a railroad depot. Access from all areas on the peninsula was practical and convenient. Business commuters to San Francisco continue to use the railway, but the race fan has generally found other means of transportation.

Bruce Campbell stood by the paddock on the grandstand side looking intensely at his horse in the fifth race. He had an Atlanta Braves cap on his head, and he wore dark blue slacks, a white shirt open at the collar, and a gray cardigan sweater. Polished black shoes were on his feet.

"Can you tell me what this asterisk next to the weight factor means?" a man next to him said. The man was middle-aged, taller than most, and dressed in dark gray slacks and an Hawaiian shirt. He spoke loudly and pointed to a section on his open program. On top of the page, attached with a paper clip, was a picture of the man on an FBI identification card.

Bruce knew the card was authentic. "It means the jockey riding that horse is an apprentice, a jockey who has not been riding for more than a year. On his horse he is allowed five pounds less than a veteran jockey."

"Thank you," the man said. "Who do you like in the race?"

"Number eight." Bruce watched the jockeys mount and the horses left the paddock on the way to the track.

"Why?"

"Toss out the last race, and he'd be one of the favorites," Bruce said. "He needed his last since he hadn't raced for six months. And his recent workouts are very good."

61

The crowd around them had dispersed and the two men stood alone. "William Fisher wants to see you, sir," the man said quietly.

"Billy Fisher?"

"I guess so, sir. I don't know him that well. He's my boss."

"I'll be damned!" Bruce said.

"He'd like you at his home for dinner tonight. Around six. Three-seventy-four Hedge Lane, Millbrae. Not far from here. Can you remember the address, and will you be able to find it? I don't want to give you the address and directions on paper. Someone could be watching," the man said.

"I'll remember, and I'll find it, but I'll bring my dog, too. She's outside in the truck," Bruce said. "Now, I got to go and bet my horse." He glanced at the small tote board near the paddock. "Number eight, Maverick, is eighteen to one. You better get on him!"

"I will, sir." The man left and went in an opposite direction.

Bruce walked quickly to a mutual clerk and placed five dollars to win on his horse, and he returned to his seat. Maverick won and paid thirty-nine dollars and forty cents.

After the races Bruce went to the parking lot. He opened the tailgate of the Suburban and removed the full bowl of water from the floor. The noise from the door awakened the dog. She woke with a start and a growl, saw her master, and sheepishly wagged her tail.

"You sleep more and more. All the time." Bruce patted the dog. "I don't blame you, though, you're getting up there and you need more rest." He looked at her paws and muzzle. "Lots of gray. Old grandma Christy, that's what we're going to call you. And another thing, you never drink any water when I leave you with George." Christy cocked her head at him. "I know, you don't want to go to the bathroom. But, we'll find one now." Bruce started the vehicle and Christy placed her head on his lap and under the right arm.

He went to a small park near the downtown sector of San Mateo. No one was at the park. Bruce placed a tennis ball in his pocket. Christy saw the movement and she danced around him when they were outside the car. He threw the ball, and he sat on a bench. He began to reminisce. He thought of the man who invited him to dinner. Billy was a student at one of his classes at Langley, Virginia. Over twenty-five years ago. Billy did well for himself in the Agency, and he remembered having worked with him, instructing him on two or three assignments. They became friends despite a seven year age difference. He nodded. I bet that's why he wants to see me, he thought. Something to do with Moroni. That old son-of-a-bitch is becoming a real bother. In the late seventies Billy was Deputy Chief at the Agency, and many thought that one day he would be the big boss. But politics became ugly and played its game. The FBI wanted him and he left the Agency and took the Bureau's district job in San Francisco. He's tough, very tough, he thought. Lays it on the line. But fair, and reliable. Unfortunately, he's too damn honest.

The house on Hedge Lane in Millbrae was a good-looking residence in an excellent neighborhood. An inviting one story home with a red brick exterior, multi-paned lead windows, and a heavy shake roof. The landscaping was meticulous. Bruce parked on the driveway, snapped a leash on Christy, and together they walked toward the front door which opened before their arrival.

"For Christ's Sake, how many years has it been?" William Fisher said. He was six foot four inches, thin, a full head of white hair, and sharp pointed features. Like his visitor, he wore slacks and a white shirt.

"A long time, Billy. A very long time," Bruce said. They hugged each other and tears were in their eyes. He studied his former student. "I don't understand how a young man like you can be sprouting all that white hair."

"It's the job, makes one old in a hurry. Besides, fifty-five isn't young anymore." Fisher kneeled and patted the Lab. "Come on in and bring Christy with you. She's very welcome."

A plump elderly woman with a pleasant smile stood in the living room. Fisher introduced her, "This is Hulda, and Hulda this is my dear friend and former boss, Bruce Campbell, and his pal, Christy. Hulda is my friend, a great cook, and looks after things around here."

Bruce shook her hand. Christy wagged her tail. Hulda giggled. "That's a nice way to say I'm Mister Fisher's housekeeper and cook," she said with a slight German accent. She patted the dog. "What can I get for you, Mister Campbell?"

"I'd like a drink, Hulda, a bourbon and seven," Bruce said. "And I'm sure Christy would enjoy a bowl of water."

"Coming right up. You have forty-five minutes before dinner, and you come with me, Christy." Hulda turned and hurried through the dining room toward the kitchen. The black Lab obediently followed her.

The men sat opposite each other on leather chairs near an unlit fireplace. A large table lamp on an expensive end table was next to each chair. A sofa and its coffee table separated the chairs. "You were married, weren't you?" Bruce said. "About the time you joined the Agency."

"We divorced five years ago. We were married over twenty-six years." There was a long pause.

"Why the divorce?" Fisher shrugged. "I don't know, a lot of reasons, I guess. You take each other for granted after awhile, and you begin to realize that you don't love each other anymore. One very good result of the marriage. We have a son that we're very proud of. He's starting a law practice in Vermont now and his mother lives nearby, close to the grandchild." He became thoughtful. "And, too, Helen never adapted to my job. We moved quite a bit, she could see the job pressures getting to me, and she kind of went along with public opinion. You know, feelings about the Agency. As you know, Bruce, the CIA is not held in high regard. They're generally thought to be bums, drug lords or conspirators, or conniving assassins. Anything for a buck or a cover-up." His face showed disgust. "Nothing could be further from the truth. The Agency has helped this country. Sure, Kennedy was a mistake but that was the Department of Treasury's responsibility, their Secret Service, but all you read or heard was CIA or FBI fault." He paused. "I guess you know I"m with the FBI now. Couldn't say no to their offer." He smiled at Bruce. "My deputy had a ten spot on that horse you gave him."

"Ten dollars? Jesus, I only had five," Bruce said. "I should get my tout percentage."

Both men laughed.

"Since my divorce I can just about afford five to win once in awhile on a real good bet."

Their drinks were served. Hulda gave Fisher his usual, a scotch and soda. She placed crackers, cheese, peanuts and cocktail napkins on the coffee table. Christy returned with Hulda to the kitchen.

"I learned about you and Elizabeth," Fisher said.

Their expressions became serious again.

"I was surprised knowing you were married thirty-five years. No more love, huh?"

"That's about it in a nutshell," Bruce said.

"And now you're living in a trailer in Oregon. Quite a change from Tahoe."

"Yes, but a pleasant change. I can honestly say that I am as content, as comfortable, and as happy in that trailer as I've ever been. And that includes living in the twenty-three hundred square foot home in Tahoe."

"Where are you staying now?" Fisher said. He stood and went to the coffee table for some peanuts.

"A trailer park in Napa. I'll be there for a few days before I return." He joined his friend at the coffee table and he placed cheese and crackers on a napkin. He sat again with a knowing smile. "But I'm sure you know that, too. You seem to know a great deal about me, Billy. The name of my dog, my divorce, how long I was married, the trailer, Oregon, my being at Bay Meadows. And all this knowledge has to do with Moroni, and the ex Mrs. Moroni. Doesn't it?"

"Yes," Fisher said, and sat down. "I guess you could say your involvement is one of circumstance and coincidence. We're out to get Moroni, and then you come along."

He shook his head and his eyes widened. "I couldn't believe it. And I had to warn you. Your life is in danger, Bruce. Moroni is wacko when it comes to his ex-wife."

"I know all that. You're not telling me anything new." Bruce leaned toward his friend, his eyes had a softness, but they were also serious.

"I love Kathryn Stevens Moroni, and there is nothing that will keep us apart." He paused. "Understood?"

"Yes, I understand. I kind of figured that," Fisher said. "But, then again, if you're not going to run, you can help us."

"I kind of figured that," Bruce said.

They both laughed again.

"But I won't help if I feel anything I say puts Kate in jeopardy," Bruce said.

"Yeah, another Catch-22," Fisher said. "Damn, if we could just get evidence, real evidence, to incriminate Moroni and put him away, but he always has an out. Fear is his big weapon. We've tried to reason and assure protection with the druggist that was hurt, but he's scared shitless. We've approached Ms. Stevens. Now that she's divorced, she could be a tremendous witness. She knows a great deal. She told us frankly and honestly that her safety is very secondary to the safety of her children, and we could interpret that as we saw fit. She would say no more, and we haven't asked her to."

Fisher studied his old friend. He had made the decision to withhold nothing. "I've infiltrated his organization. I felt that when his personal vendetta became paramount I had a shot at him. I have a chance to catch him with his pants down, and I want to know what he's thinking. We've concentrated on Moroni for the past two years and we're no closer to getting him than when we started. And, now, attrition will probably take over. Then I'd go after DeLucci."

"You're involved very personally. Aren't you?"

"Yes, I am."

"What do you mean by this attrition?" Bruce said.

"First, let me give you some background." Fisher stood and went behind his chair. He leaned on it with his elbows. "Moroni is the godfather. He's big. The biggest. Practically everything illegal can be connected to Moroni's family or organization. Drugs, prostitution are only part of it. With the legality of lotteries throughout the country and watch and wager racing in almost every state, the family has lost many millions of dollars. They now own five casinos in Las Vegas, six in other parts of Nevada, and two in Atlantic City"

He went for the peanuts again. "And the son-of-a-bitch has come up with a monster. Think about this. Abortions are legal but embarrassing and sometimes dangerous for the pregnant woman to go to a legal clinic. Picket lines are common and a patient can be identified, and violence at these centers has been known. So what does he do? He buys homes, residences, all over the country, and places a doctor and a nurse there to perform abortions. No sign, no plaque, just a nice home in a pretty subdivision, but the words out in the right places. I hear they think abortions will eventually be illegal.

"Then, bigger bucks! And we've also heard that these same doctors are going to be medically available to terminally ill patients for suicide assistance." He sat again. "At a nice price, of course. Tens of thousands of terminally ill people out there in considerable pain who will have the opportunity to go to their death peacefully just like the dog they had put to sleep. They're money to these manipulators who encourage the patient. By encourage, I mean 'having the guts to die'. Evil, but a smart son-of-a-bitch. The bastard has become mental, you know."

"Go on," Bruce said.

"DeLucci, protege and next in line, and the family are very concerned over this personal vendetta. Moroni has become old and weak and obviously mentally unstable. They are concerned that he has become vulnerable to detection. They are thinking that they want him out and we feel that soon he'll be given an opportunity to resign. I don't think he would have much choice."

"Then what?" Bruce said.

"He's vulnerable now, that's what!" Fisher said. He stood, put his hands in his pockets, and walked around in front of Bruce. "I want to get Moroni and possibly DeLucci involvement now before he's out. With those two gone I'm sure the family would begin to deteriorate. They're the brains, particularly Moroni. Otherwise, if Moroni retires, I go after a younger DeLucci in complete control and in agreement with the old methods."

Hulda entered the living room. Christy was with her. "Dinner is served, it's all on the table. And the food is getting cold, so you better come." She smiled, turned and hurried toward the kitchen. Christy was close behind her.

The two men sat at the dining room table and enjoyed the anticipation of what they saw. Dinner consisted of prime rib, generally medium rare, Yorkshire pudding, mashed potatoes, brown gravy, tiny peas, German style red cabbage, and home made biscuits. Dessert consisted of home baked cherry pie with ice cream. The pie was served hot. During the meal their conversation rarely ceased and both realized how much they had missed the friendship.

They had dessert and coffee in the living room. Both remained quiet for several minutes enjoying a silent companionship and savoring Hulda's meal. Christy lay in front of the coffee table. Fisher became thoughtful, and he looked worried. His face was apologetic. "I have to tell you something now that is embarrassing and difficult for me to admit. Bear in mind, only recently was I aware of your relationship with Kathryn Stevens. You are going to be meeting a man --"

Christy stood and growled at the front door. Several moments elapsed before the doorbell sounded.

"That's probably him now," Fisher said.

Hulda answered the front door.

A short man wearing glasses and a mustache was ushered into the room. He was quite heavy, bald, thirty-five, and very well dressed in a suit and tie. "Bruce," Fisher said, "I'd like you to meet Homer Higginbottom, one of our agents, and in my opinion one of our best. Homer, this is Bruce Campbell."

Bruce Campbell was introduced to Smitty.

They shook hands.

"I've heard a great deal about you, sir," Homer said.

Bruce smiled. "No sir, please. Bruce and Homer, is that okay?"

"Fine."

"And take that damn coat and tie off," Fisher insisted. "You make me look too informal in my own house."

"Well, sir, when you meet the boss, go to his home and all, I thought --" He saw the scowl. Homer removed his coat and took off his tie. He sat on the sofa.

Hulda brought him coffee and hot cherry pie ala mode. Christy sat beside him, all attention.

"And Homer is the infiltrator?" Bruce said to Fisher.

Fisher nodded. "You're way ahead of me. Yes, he is, for almost two years now. Homer's had a hard time. Being around Moroni, with instructions and all, it's difficult not to become a criminal. Temptation can lead to crime, too. Isn't that right, Homer?" Fisher smiled.

"Yes, sir." He looked at Bruce. "Is it okay if I give Christy the last of my dessert?"

"It's okay with me if it's okay with the boss here. She'll be eating off one of his plates."

"It's perfectly all right," Fisher said.

They watched Homer gulp down his last bite and place the plate on the carpet. There was a small piece of pie left with a tiny lump of ice cream.

The treat disappeared immediately. Christy returned to her spot in front of the coffee table.

"You know, just a couple of weeks ago our friend here gave the Bureau five thousand Moroni bonus dollars. Isn't that right, Homer?"

"Yes, sir, for services rendered. I almost kept the money, though, figuring even you would never know about it. But, damn it, I would have known and -- Ah, the hell with it."

"What kind of services?" Bruce said.

Homer looked at his boss.

"Tell him," Fisher said. "Whatever he wants to know. I'll be glad when this is over. I've been worried about it."

Homer spoke directly to Bruce. "Moroni wanted me to keep an eye on his ex-wife. I followed her to Oregon. To your trailer by the river. He's a fanatic about her, particularly if he feels she is going to get sexually involved. He insisted on all the details."

"What did you tell him?" Bruce said.

"All the details, sir, explicitly. I told him about the sexual sounds coming from the trailer, and all about your lovemaking one night on a blanket in the yard when the moon was out."

"Where were you?"

"Near you, or behind a tree, or near the trailer, but not close enough for the dogs to hear," Homer said. "I didn't know who you were at the time. I know who the dogs are. I heard their names called. When I got back, Charlie Dobbs told me your name and I reported this to Mister Fisher. And, here we are. I can't be seen anywhere near our San Francisco office, and Mister Fisher wanted me to make a report to you also."

"I'm sincerely sorry about this invasion of your privacy. This very intimate privacy," Fisher said. "Homer has to be accepted and trusted by Moroni, and he did what he was told --"

"I know that, Billy. But I'd think that an area that is almost a wilderness, and late at night, would offer us whatever privacy we wanted," Bruce said calmly. "I have to admit I'm embarrassed, for Kate mostly, but don't you guys fret about it. Goddamn, where do you have to go to get away from these kooks?"

"Our files will not reveal any of the sexual details. Only that Homer followed Ms. Stevens to Oregon and that she had an affair with a man there. Your name will be mentioned, but that's all," Fisher said.

"Mister Campbell, you have to be very careful now," Homer said. "I found out from Charlie that Moroni wants you hurt bad, or killed. He doesn't care. One of us is watching Ms. Steven's home day and night waiting for your arrival, but I don't know who will be sent to do the job on you."

"Have you seen her, yet? Since you've been down here?" Fisher said.

"No, Kate is in Southern California right now, visiting her son." Bruce smiled. "He's starting med-school and she wants to make sure he's comfortable in his new apartment. She'll be back in a couple of days and I'll be seeing her."

"Go back to Oregon, Bruce. Now. Let this thing cool off for a few months." Fisher saw the look, and he shook his head. "I knew you wouldn't. I know you pretty well, and I knew. Can I say anything that'll change your mind?"

"No."

"I can't protect you, Bruce."

"I know that. I kind of figured Moroni would be after me. You haven't surprised me, only your surveillance of me." Bruce chuckled and shook his head. "What the hell, I can't do anything about it."

"Isn't that sweet." Fisher sounded mad. "Don't be so heroic, and glib. You're standing at death's door!"

No one spoke.

"Do you have a weapon?" Fisher was calmer. "You don't have to worry about a license, I'll take care of that."

"A twenty-five caliber Bareta. A nine fifty with silencer," Bruce said.

"You need something bigger," Fisher said.

"It'll do the job, and it's easy to carry around. And that's all I ever wanted."

Fisher took two four by five black and white photographs from an envelope off a side table and handed them to Bruce.

71

"The picture on your right is Charlie Dobbs, Moroni's number one man."

"Kate's dad told me a little bit about him," Bruce said.

"The other man is a walking weapon. Mean and tough. A Filipino, Roy Machato. I think one of these guys will be your man, but I'm not sure. It will be a big help if I know who it is with a full description. His body would do, but then we couldn't interrogate him, of course."

"I'm glad you have such confidence in me," Bruce said.

"I don't, really. You're too fucking old for this sort of thing."

Bruce nodded casually. A few moments elapsed. "Thank you," he said. "Thank you both. You've done all you can. And you, Homer, watch yourself. You take good care of yourself."

"I will, sir, but you watch out, too. You hear?" Homer had a softness in his tone.

"Homer, it's time we think about getting you out of that environment. We're pushing our luck," Fisher said. "We might get you conveniently killed. We'll send you and your family away for awhile."

"Alive, I hope, sir!"

They all laughed.

"Alive, Homer, and with a promotion, too," Fisher said.

"How big is your family, Homer?"

"My wife, Laura, and two children, Susan, eleven, and Bill, nine. Bill was named after my boss. Laura says the kids are really smart. Tops in their class," Homer said proudly.

"How often have you been able to see them?" Bruce said sadly.

"Four times, briefly, in the last twenty-two months."

"It's time you got out, Homer. Check back with me in one week," Fisher said.

"I will, sir." Homer put on his coat, and picked up his tie. He nodded at William Fisher. He shook Bruce's hand. "I really enjoyed meeting you, sir. And, Christy."

"Thank you, Homer. Take care of yourself."

"Goodnight, gentlemen." Homer let himself out the front door.

"That's the kind of work that can cause a divorce," Bruce said.

"I know," Fisher said glumly.

Christy had wandered to the closed drapes that were over the front window. She poked her head between the drapes, and she looked outside.

Homer was walking the brick pathway to a car by the curb. He did not notice the man crouched behind the vehicle in front of a neighbors property. The man was Charlie Dobbs. He got in his car and followed Smitty's car down the street.

Christy growled softly. A growl that no one heard.

Chapter Eight

The time was nearly midnight and Charlie Dobbs was busy making a sandwich. The cook had gone to bed but he found what he wanted in the refrigerator. He also discovered rye bread and he made two Swiss cheese sandwiches with red onion, lettuce, and mayonnaise. He prepared a side plate with radishes, dill pickle, macaroni, two sliced hard boiled eggs, and he poured himself a large glass of skim milk. He had a long day with very little to eat and he was hungry. He sat at a table in an alcove off the large kitchen and he ate with relish. The meal was gone within ten minutes. He burped loudly, stood, and went to a wall and pressed one of its buttons.

The speaker on the same wall emitted static, but a voice could be heard. "Yes, what is it?"

Dobbs pressed another button. "Get into the kitchen," he said to the speaker.

"Do you realize it's after midnight?" the voice on the other end said.

"Roy, I don't give a shit what time it is. Get your ass in here. Now!" Dobbs said.

He went to the refrigerator and poured another glass of milk. He opened the freezer and saw a half gallon of vanilla ice cream. He prepared a large dish of the ice cream and poured nearly a half can of chocolate syrup over it.

He was nearly finished with the dessert when Roy came into the kitchen and went to the alcove.

"Well, what is it that you want?" Roy said indignantly.

Dobbs gave him a long look. "Go upstairs and wake the old man," he said quietly. "Tell him that I need to talk to him. That it's important."

"It had better be important at this time of night." Roy sounded angry.

Dobbs left his chair and hurled his body against the Filipino. Roy was flung backward against a wall and a hand was on his left wrist pulling his arm behind him and upward. He was forced to turn around and his face was pushed hard against the wall.

"Come on, puke," Dobbs said. "Show me your great judo ability."

A forty-five was in his right hand and it was pushed into Roy's right ear. "Come on, make a move so I can blow your puke face all over this room."

"Please, Charlie, you're hurting me," Roy said.

"Please, Charlie. Please, Charlie. Now, that's much better," Dobbs said. "Remember, puke face, you got two bosses. That man upstairs and me. And whatever or whenever we tell you to do something, you do it. No back talk. Do you understand me?" He pushed the left arm a little higher.

"Yes, yes, I understand. Please, you're breaking my arm."

"Please what?" Dobbs said to the back of his head.

"Please, Charlie!" The Filipino almost wept from the pain.

"Please, Charlie what?" Dobbs continued the pressure.

"Please, Charlie, sir!"

"That's more like it!" Dobbs gave him a hard shove against the wall and released him. He returned the gun to his chest holster and casually turned his back on the Filipino. He sat. "Now go upstairs and do what I told you to do."

Roy walked meekly toward the dining room but its swinging door was open and Vincent Moroni was in a wheelchair planted within the door frame.

"That won't be necessary, Roy. As you can see I'm here and Charlie and I can talk now." Moroni's smile was directed at Dobbs. "I heard noises downstairs at this odd hour and I thought I had better investigate."

His attention focused on Roy now. "You know, Roy, one of these days you're going to have the opportunity to demonstrate your judo and karate abilities. When that happens I'm sure Charlie will think more highly of you. Isn't that right, Charlie?"

"Whatever you say, Mister Moroni." Dobbs was surprised seeing his employer downstairs until he remembered the elevator

75

on the staircase attached to the banister, and a second wheelchair near the bottom landing.

"And would you like to demonstrate your ability, Roy?" the old man said.

"Yes, Mister Moroni, I would like to do that very much," Roy said.

"Good, good. Now, Roy, you go back to bed and get a good night's rest," the old man said kindly.

"Good night, Mr. Moroni," Roy said courteously. Good night, Charlie, sir." There was a tinge of bitterness in the voice. He left the room quickly.

Moroni wheeled to the table where Dobbs sat. "He won't forget this little incident."

"He's not worth a shit if he does, Mister Moroni," Charlie said.

"Yes, yes." The old man laughed quietly. "Well, now, what is it that is so important?"

"Smitty is an FBI agent," Dobbs said calmly. He saw the look on Moroni's face change to disbelief, then anger, then composure. "He's working out of the San Francisco office. The boss there is a William Fisher. Smitty reports directly to him."

"I've heard of this Fisher. He's been trying to get me indicted. He's never had any evidence, and he never will." Moroni looked at the floor for several moments. He raised his head. "Give me all the details. How did you discover him?"

"I put Smitty on night duty watching her home for the return of Campbell. When he got off duty he kept asking me questions. I told him that you wanted Campbell hurt, beat up, but he kept asking me who was going to do the job and would it be done as soon as Campbell arrived." Dobbs became aware that he was still sitting in front of his employer. He stood and tried to look natural with his hands folded in front of him.

"I became suspicious and gave him a couple of days off, telling him that he had done good work, and that he deserved some time off. I followed him the morning he left here." Dobbs talked in a monotone, but he was comfortable knowing he had facts.

"He went to a house in Petaluma and used a key to get inside," Dobbs said. "Within a couple of hours a woman about his age came outside the house with two children, a boy and a girl, about nine or ten. We've known this about him, about his woman, children, and where he lived. But that night, day before yesterday, Smitty left the house a little after eight, dressed in a suit and tie, and I followed him to a house in Millbrae. In the driveway was Campbell's truck. He was in there about an hour and when he left I followed him back to his house in Petaluma."

Moroni's attentive eyes were like slits on his face. His chair and body never moved.

"When the lights went out there I drove back to the Millbrae house," Dobbs said. "Campbell and his black dog left there about one in the morning. That damn dog barked at my car and started toward it but Campbell got the dog in his truck. I waited there and about seven in the morning a man with white hair and in a business suit left the house and got in his car. I followed him to San Francisco. We left our cars in a parking garage and I followed him to the FBI office. I learned from a security guard in the building that his name is William Fisher, the boss there. I then drove back to the Petaluma house. Smitty's car was where he left it. I stayed there for the rest of the day and up until about three hours ago. Not much activity. Smitty should be back here this morning. That's it, Mister Moroni."

The old man had a blank expression for several moments. Suddenly, he became aware of Dobbs. "You have done excellent work, Charlie, and you are very loyal. I appreciate that and I'll show my appreciation, believe me." He became thoughtful. "The woman and children, are they Smitty's family?"

"I would think so, Mister Moroni, but I don't know for sure. But I'll find out," Dobbs said, still standing with his hands folded.

"That's not necessary. In any case, she's a confidant," Moroni said. He became pensive for several moments. "Was

Smitty ever aware of this pharmacist in Sonoma?" he said. "The one who went out with her."

"Yes, I told him about the guy. He was with us only a few weeks then and I told him about beating him up, scaring the hell out of him, and why. And that he left town. Smitty was one of the ones watching her and my telling him was all part of why it was important. At the time, the information was just normal talk. I wasn't suspicious then." Dobbs put his hands in his pants pockets. He looked worried.

"That's alright, Charlie, you did no wrong. Have you ever told Smitty about any other jobs that I've given you, or about any other activity within the organization?"

"No," Dobbs said. "I might have skirted a thing or two, but nothing definite. That I'm sure of, Mister Moroni."

Moroni turned his wheelchair around and went to the refrigerator. He removed a small bowl of custard and a spoon from a drawer. He ate tiny amounts, continually staring at the bowl until it was empty. He placed the bowl on the tile counter. "We must act quickly, but I must think on it awhile. We must be sure that we've covered everything. I will have two or three jobs for you. I want you to personally handle this, so stay close. I know now that Smitty's job has to be a little different. We will not tolerate traitors or spies, and we must make that quite clear. I will get back to you. Good night."

The old man started to wheel from the kitchen. He stopped and turned around. "By the way, Charlie, how did you get the name William Fisher out of a security guard?"

"The security guard is a she," Dobbs said. "When she was on break at the candy counter I bought her a candy bar and kidded her about the handsome man with the white hair that she made eyes at. She laughed like a mule and told me that he could never be interested in her and she told me his name and position. I figured I could get away with flirting with her. She's an ugly bitch."

The old man stared at him. "Amazing. Never leave me, Charlie. Never leave me!" He wheeled around but suddenly

78

turned back again. "And, Charlie, let's find out more about this Campbell. Check into his background."

"Yes, Mister Moroni."

Chapter Nine

As one approached Moroni's two story English Tudor estate, the five car garage was located to the left of the residence. The garage was attached to the house but angled at about forty-five degrees toward the back of the house. One garage door was open and the rear of an older Chevrolet sedan could be seen. Two large fluorescent light fixtures glared from the ceiling. Charlie Dobbs opened the trunk and inspected the storage space making sure there were no obstructions or unnecessary baggage. He went to a worktable in the garage and took a body bag and placed it behind the spare tire in the trunk. He returned to the table and opened a large storage drawer and removed two bundles of dynamite. There were several sticks in each bundle and each was wired to a timing device. He put the dynamite in an empty cardboard box, opened the rear door of the sedan, and placed the box on the floor. He returned to the table and removed from the same drawer thirty feet of new white rope and he put the rope on the floor of the car. He went to the back of the garage and took a shovel that was attached to a Peg-Board. He placed the shovel over the other articles on the floor. The length of the shovel was longer than the width of the vehicle and the top of its handle rested on the rear seat. He repeated this operation with a comb rake. He took a box of garbage bags off the table and placed the box on the car floor. He closed the door but left the trunk open. He glanced at his watch. The time was 9 p.m.

Smitty entered the garage. "Hello, Charlie."

Dobbs went to the wall by the garage entrance to the house and pressed a button. The garage door closed.

"I'm surprised you wanted me here this time of night," Smitty said. "I'd normally be in Sonoma watching her house for the past two hours."

Dobbs took a pair of tight fitting latex gloves from a box on the table. He pulled them over his hands and placed the box on the car floor on the passenger side of the front seat.

"Why the gloves, Charlie?"

"Dirty work ahead."

"When do I go back to watching the ex-Moroni babe?" Smitty said.

Dobbs approached Smitty. "You don't go back. Your job is finished. In fact, Mister FBI agent, you're finished." Suddenly, he kicked him hard in the crotch, the blow landing directly on Smitty's testicles.

Smitty went to his knees, his head rocking back and forth to the pavement. He groaned pathetically. "Jesus. Goddamn. My God, it hurts. Charlie, give--, this up. We'll pay-, well for, your evidence. No strings, you're free." He began to cough. He vomited part of his dinner.

"What's paying well, Mister Agent?" Dobbs said.

"Half a--, million, Charlie. Really."

"No, that wouldn't be right. The old man has been very good to me. He always pays me well. I don't need your fucking half million. Besides, you're a lying son-of-a-bitch!"

Dobbs reached behind with his right hand. From beneath his windbreaker he pulled out an iron pipe. He hit Smitty on the back of the head with the pipe.

Dobbs bent over the body that was still breathing. He examined the head wound. He went to the table and took gauze and hospital tape and returned to the body and bandaged the head feeling certain that no blood would seep. The table supplied a large piece of transparent plastic which he carefully placed throughout the interior of the trunk. He completely stripped the body. He took four pieces of rope, each fifteen inches long, a roll of duct tape, and one garbage bag from the table. He tied Smitty's hands behind his back using two pieces of rope. He tied the ankles together using the other two pieces. He used duct tape on the bandage and went around the head and over the mouth three times. He made sure the nostrils were clear. He picked up the body and deposited it into the trunk and arranged the plastic sheeting. He made sure the trunk lid would close over the body and he closed the trunk. He searched Smitty's clothes and found a set of keys which he pocketed. The wallet contained eighty-six dollars which he kept. He picked up Smitty's clothes, the shoes, and the iron pipe, and put them in the bag along with the wallet. He placed the bag on the rear seat of the car. He also placed a tool box in the car, a new inexpensive four piece plastic raincoat, a plastic gallon bottle of drinking water, a bar of soap, and a large bath towel. He cleaned the blood and vomit off the concrete floor using a bucket of water, tri-sodium phosphate, a stiff brush, and a mop. He broke the mop in half with his knee and placed the two halves, the bucket and the brush in another bag. He removed the latex gloves and put them in the bag, and the bag also went on the rear seat of the car. He used the side entrance from the garage to the house and went to the half bath nearby to urinate and wash his hands, and he made sure no blood was on his person. He returned to the garage and got into the car on the driver's side. He started the engine and used the automatic garage door opener to open the garage. He backed the car out and used the remote to close the garage.

Charlie Dobbs turned the car onto the estate driveway and he drove through the opening at the wrought iron gates and into a quiet residential street. He took street after street in the Hillsborough area until he reached a wider road that took him to the freeway. He hummed a tune from Snow White, 'Whistle While You Work'. He knew of a nice all-night restaurant just off the freeway in San Rafael. He had plenty of time for a good meal before they reached Petaluma.

Dobbs looked at his watch. The time was 2 a.m. He got out of the car, opened the rear door and picked up the paper carton. He carried the carton to the front porch of the home across the street from where he parked. He put the carton down and removed Smitty's keys from his pocket. He turned the lock slowly and quietly let himself into the dark living room. A low wattage night light burned in the hallway. He quietly opened a door off the hallway. He peered inside and two children were asleep in twin beds. He closed the door. An open door was at the end of the hallway that led to a bathroom. One other door remained in the hallway of the small home. As he began to open the door he heard the forced air furnace ignite and warm air began to flow on him from a vent near the ceiling. He looked inside and saw an attractive middle-aged woman laying nude on her back on top of a disheveled bed. She was asleep.

"Goddamn cunt," he thought, "laying nude like that with her children in the next room. What if they had to get up in the middle of the night and needed her. Imagine seeing her like that. Jesus."

His eyes examined her body and an erection started. The woman had a large pubic area, her thick black hair reaching her navel. Her breasts were enormous, drooping over the sides of her rib cage. His penis was throbbing and as he moved toward the woman he unzipped his fly and fumbled for his penis, but he had difficulty getting the organ through the opening in his underwear and the fly. He stopped. The penis was in his hand and his closed fist encircled half of it. He knew fucking her would probably wake the children and the job would be easier if all of them remained asleep, but his cock wouldn't cooperate. He took two steps backward, and continued to look at the woman. He began to masturbate. Within a minute, semen spurted and large gobs landed on a nightstand and the shade of a lamp. He zipped his fly shut. He felt much better and he was ready to go to work.

Charlie Dobbs brought the dynamite inside the house. By the hallway light he set the detonators and the timing devices. He placed one bundle of dynamite under the woman's bed, and the other bundle by the door to the children's bedroom. He was in the living room on his way out when he saw what he thought was a photograph on a table. He removed a pocket flashlight from his jacket and shined the light on the color photograph of a young Smitty and the woman in tuxedo and wedding dress.

83

They held hands. A narrow nameplate was on the bottom of the frame, and it read, 'Introducing Mister and Mrs. Homer Higginbottom'.

"Can you imagine that, Homer Higginbottom!" Dobbs mumbled. "With a name like that the fuckhead had to be queer. Probably had to marry the broad to get into the FBI. She's better off without him!" He snapped off the light and went out the front, quietly closing the door behind him.

Dobbs drove the car one block down the street and again parked. He looked at his watch. He leaned back on the seat and quietly hummed the Snow White tune. Ten minutes later he turned around and looked up the street. In a few moments a tremendous explosion was heard, and a fire started. Lights began popping in the homes on the street. He started the car and drove slowly from the commotion.

He turned onto a side road that was paved but narrowed to a dirt road when it neared the water's edge of San Andreas Lake. The lake abutted the western side of a freeway in an area that was a mile west of Millbrae. He parked within a small grove of trees and turned off the headlights. When he opened the trunk its light came on and Homer's eyes were open and frightened.

Dobbs removed the body bag from the spare tire area. He unzipped the bag and, like stuffing an envelope, he put Homer sideways into the bag. He turned the body so his face looked out the opening. He retrieved the white rope from the car and at one end tied Homer's feet securely together after he removed the smaller pieces of rope. He put on the plastic raincoat which included a covering for his shoes, a jacket and pants, and a hood. He put on another pair of gloves. He removed the duct tape from Homers head and mouth, the bandage on his head, and he began to remove the rope from around his wrists.

Homer shivered. "What was that explosion, Charlie?" he stuttered.

"Your house blowing up along with your kids and broad," Dobbs said, removing the rope from Homer's wrists.

"Oh, My, My God!" Homer's bladder and bowels lost control.

"You know, Smitty, or should I say Homer Higginbottom?" Dobbs laughed softly. "Higginbottom. You couldn't pick a worse name. Anyway, that woman of yours really had some pussy. And the tits. God, I really wanted to fuck her. But I didn't, Homer. Homer." He laughed a little louder.

Homer was crying and the tears caused a coughing seizure. Mucous ran from his nostrils.

"Damn, but you stink. But you don't have to put up with your shit anymore. I do, that's what I get paid for." Dobbs displayed a narrow six inch blade from a switchblade knife. "So long, Homer." He held Homer's head back with his left hand and he slowly slit the throat from under the right ear to the left ear. The blood slowly erupted but in a moment a miniature red waterfall gushed freely.

Homer's eyes gradually lost their life and then they stared at nothing. A few gurgles and some blood came from the mouth.

Dobbs cut off Homer's penis and from the soft spot just above the gaping wound he slowly cut the stomach open and continued past the sternum to the cut neck. With his hands he widened the cut. He made sure urine, bowel movement, the penis, the blood, and the entrails, that were beginning to expand from the stomach, still remained confined to the body bag. He placed the rope at the feet and closed the bag. He removed the bloody gloves, placed them on the plastic sheeting, and closed the trunk lid.

Dobbs took off his plastic hood and examined it and the rest of the raincoat for blood. There were a few spatters on the jacket and upper pants. From the gallon jug, he poured water on the end of the bath towel and wiped the blood, and dried with the other end of the towel. He put the towel and water jug into another bag and placed it in the car. He started the car and left the area.

His watch read 4:05 a.m. The car idled on the shoulder of Millbrae Avenue just east of the overpass on the Bayshore

Freeway. A new set of latex gloves grasped the steering wheel as Dobbs looked carefully behind him and in front of him. No cars were on the avenue. He searched south and north on the freeway and no cars were noticeable. One small headlight was seen in the far distance. The vehicle moved forward rapidly and he shifted to the second gear. The car came to a screeching halt in the middle of the overpass on the north side of the avenue. Dobbs quickly got out of the car, opened the trunk, zipped a small opening in the body bag to remove the rope, and shut the bag. He carried the bag to the top of the concrete railing and put it down. He placed the end of the rope through one of the decorative opening in the concrete and over the top of the railing, next to the bag, around and through again, tying it securely. He opened the bag fully and pulled Homer's head and shoulders from the top of the bag. Holding the bag at the end of the opening he turned over the bag. The contents fell toward the pavement on the freeway. The body, head first, was at the end of the rope a few feet above the freeway. The neck was broken and the body swayed for a long time.

With the help of the railing, Dobbs turned the bag inside out over the freeway making sure all contents had dropped. He placed the bag in the trunk. He took off his raincoat gear and the rubber gloves and put them in the trunk and closed the lid. He drove away using the Millbrae Avenue on ramp that took him to the freeway, south, to San Jose. The time was 4:09 a.m.

Dobbs enjoyed a large breakfast with three cups of coffee and he still had time to investigate the area where the drugstore was located. He felt sure none of the employees would arrive before seven-thirty, and he was particularly interested in knowing the location of their parking area.

He went to a Longs Drugs on a corner near downtown San Jose, sixty miles south of San Francisco. He discovered parking was prohibited behind the drugstore, only refuse containers and delivery trucks were allowed. He was almost certain the employees parked in the customers area, but they probably were not allowed to park immediately in front of the store. He

86

gambled and chose a parking row about forty yards from the store entrance. At 8:45 a.m. his man arrived not far from where he was parked.

Using the rear partition of the man's car as a shield Dobbs lowered his head and went to the back of the car and waited for the door to open. When it did, Dobbs moved quickly. He held his hand in his jacket pocket. "Johnny, baby," he said quietly to the man. "Get out of your car."

"Good God, it's you again." The man got out of the car.

"Uh, huh," Dobbs uttered. "Now close your door and lock your car." The man hesitated but the fear in his eyes was evident. Dobbs knew that now was the best chance the man had to escape. There were a few people in the area and some could be witness to a killing. The man could scream and run and Dobbs couldn't do anything about it. Too much time between here and his car and the getaway and someone could take a license number or make an identification. He knew his man was afraid. Fear was on his side, and he noticed a slight tremble of the legs. Most of his targets had just folded and their fear was the only emotion. "Do what I say, or this gun in my pocket will blow your fucking head off."

The man closed the door and locked the car.

Dobbs jerked his head toward his car. "Head for that car, the only one in the row, and get behind the steering wheel."

The man did as he was told.

Dobbs sat on the passenger side. He withdrew his hand from the jacket, opened the car pocket under the dashboard, and removed a forty-five hand gun. He had an evil and loud laugh. "There was no gun outside, asshole. But now there is!" He leveled the gun at the man. "Start the car and go one-oh-one South, and drive carefully."

The man, John Haversack, a pharmacist, fifty years old, thin, five foot ten, light sandy colored hair, gaunt face, was very scared. He was beaten by Dobbs in Sononta nearly two years ago. Although he missed Kate's friendship, his fear of violence and harm was greater than his affection.

Twenty-three miles south of San Jose and north of Gilroy, Dobbs directed John to make a left turn on a narrow paved road. They went five miles and made a right turn on a lonely dirt road. They went another two miles and drove off the road. The driver was directed to park behind a grouping of large boulders. The area was remote. No foot or vehicular traffic was evident.

"You know I haven't told anyone anything about what you did to me," the voice trembled. "I've had the opportunity to talk to the FBI and I kept my mouth shut, and I'm going to keep it shut."

"Good for you, Johnny baby. But we can't take a chance on you. Get out of the car!" Dobbs ordered.

John got out of the car. "I'm going to be married next month."

"Wrong, Johnny, you were going to be married next month." Dobbs took the shovel from the backseat and with the tip of the shovel made a line in the loamy soil two feet wide and six feet long. "Dig within those lines." He handed John the shovel. "Now!"

John began to weep. "Please don't kill me. I've done you no harm. Please!"

"Shut the fuck up, and dig, or you'll be digging with your head caved in!" Dobbs was enjoying himself.

Forty minutes later John stood in the hole, his waistline level with the topography.

"Keep digging," Dobbs said.

Dobbs went to the car and opened the trunk and again donned the four piece plastic raincoat. He put on a new pair of plastic gloves and then looked at the hole being dug. He didn't see John. "What the shit!" He ran to the hole with the gun in hand.

A spade full of soil hit Dobbs fully in the face. He sputtered and coughed. The sandy soil irritated his eyes and nostrils and he gasped for air. His sight was momentarily impaired.

John slowly climbed out of the hole but his entire body trembled. He looked around. He had left the shovel in the hole.

He pounced on the gun in Dobbs' hand and tried to wrestle it free. He was no match for Dobbs who began to see better. Dobbs pulled the gun from John's grasp and hit the back of his head with the barrel. John fell forward on his face.

Dobbs spit several times and rubbed his eyes. "I got to work on this guy but I don't want to get bit," he mumbled. "And I don't want to work with blood on the front of his body." He snapped the switchblade open and carefully shoved the blade between ribs and into the heart.

John Haversack, a pharmacist, grunted and died instantly.

Dobbs found a sturdy stick and broke it to usable size. He went to the car and returned with the tool box. He turned the man over and forced his mouth open. He pushed the stick deep into the mouth and placed it between the upper palate and tongue. He opened the tool box and removed a dentist's pliers, claw pliers, a heavy flat headed screwdriver, and he would use his knife.

Dobbs took over an hour to remove all the man's teeth. He was clumsy at the job. Blood, gums, and teeth soon looked alike.

Using both hands, Dobbs used a shear to cut off the man's fingers and thumbs. He placed them in a small bag.

Dobbs stripped the body. He removed the man's wallet and keys, and he looked for other identification but found none. He kept the forty-seven dollars from the wallet. He reached down and got the shovel and then pushed the man's body into the grave. He first shoveled the bloody soil into the grave, and then he filled the grave. He got the comb rake from the car and he raked and shoveled the excess soil over a wide area until the grave was level. He scattered leaves, rocks, and pebbles over the grave site and surrounding area. He was satisfied.

Dobbs took off the rain gear and dumped everything into the green bags on the backseat of the car, including the plastic sheeting and body bag in the trunk. He kept the forty-five making sure there was no blood on the gun. He broke the shovel and rake in half and put them in a fresh bag with another bag pulled over the top. He removed the gloves and used the water and soap to clean his hands, face, and neck, and he dried himself with the towel. He inspected himself and the car for blood or tissue. He emptied the water bottle on the ground and placed the bottle, towel, soap, and the dirty gloves into a bag.

He drove from the site. The time was 12:45 p.m.

Early the next morning public containers of refuse were emptied by the county at curbside in some parts of San Mateo. On a quiet cul-de-sac, Charlie Dobbs had deposited his used bags in a partially filled container.

Chapter Ten

Napa, California. Two days later.

Twenty-seven children came to his trailer site yesterday evening on Halloween. Bruce had kept count and he was pleased that he had bought a variety and enough candy for each child to have an ample amount. There were a few pieces of Hershey Kisses left for him to share with Christy.

The day had been clear and beautiful, but cool. The sun had already set but Bruce remained sitting on the patio under the trailer awning wearing an old beat-up sweater, denim trousers, and the badly marked white tennis shoes. He sipped a glass of wine. Christy lay nearby. The light from the kitchen illuminated the patio. He enjoyed looking at all the trailers, the street lights, the well maintained grounds and landscaping, and the pool nearby where underwater lights played magic with the surface.

The trailer park was beautiful with a top rating. It should be, he thought. He was paying twenty-three dollars per day which included two dollars for Christy. The amount was high compared to his rent and environment in Tiller, but this place was very modern and nice, and only twenty-five minutes from Kate in Sonoma.

Except for the last two evenings, they had been together every day and night since Kate's return from Southern California. They loved each other very much. He had never realized that love could be so perfect, so very wonderful. They spent a great deal of time in bed and their lovemaking was uninhibited, comfortable, and relaxing. And he knew that their relationship was more than sexual. They enjoyed being together, communicating, laughing, and each wanting to please the other.

Kate had handed Bruce an article from a Santa Rosa newspaper on a book review. Two psychologists co-authored a book on what constituted a successful and happy marriage. "Read it," Kate said, "I'm sure you'll agree. I do. It says it all."

Glenn Mathews

The article revealed that there are three necessary ingredients in a successful marriage. Should one of them be missing the marriage would be unhappy and probably end in divorce. Should two or three of these requirements be missing, the marriage would be a disaster. The article condensed and indicated the three ingredients: a physical intimacy enjoyed by each partner; a commitment to one another and family; and an abiding friendship with one another.

Bruce had agreed.

Christy growled when car headlights turned into their site and parked alongside George in front of the trailer. The growl became a bark, and then several loud harsh barks until the car's occupant appeared. The tail wagged. Their visitor was William Fisher, and he was alone.

The two men shook hands. Bruce saw sorrow in his friend's eyes. Fisher was about to speak.

"Don't say anything just yet," Bruce said. "You look like you've been through hell. I'll fix you a scotch and soda, take a couple of steaks down and thaw them in the microwave. You sit and relax outside here with Christy. I'll be right back."

He returned in a few minutes with the drink and he had refilled the wine glass. Bruce sat beside his friend. He waited for Fisher to take a couple of swallows from his drink.

"What is it, Billy?" he said.

"Homer's dead." Fisher looked out at the night. "Did you see the front-page picture in the Chronicle yesterday?"

Bruce nodded. "The man hanging from the overpass, eviscerated." The eyebrows lifted and the lines on his forehead deepened. "That was Homer?"

"Yes, but that's not all. Earlier, his home in Petaluma was blown to smithereens. His wife and two children, just a few pieces of bone and blood spattered on lumber." William Fisher began to cry softly. Tears rolled down his cheeks. "I can't take anymore of this shit, Bruce, I can't take anymore. I thought I'd seen it all, but this." His head shook slowly, and anguish was on his face. "All so unnecessary." He began to sob.

92

They sat in silence. The sobbing eventually stopped. Fisher wiped his face with a handkerchief. "I'm sorry, I didn't mean to do that. I --"

"I understand, Billy. Believe it or not, I've had to cry over a similar situation. Although, I don't think I've ever been around anything this brutal. Moroni?"

"Yes, it's that piece of shit and his fucking henchman, Charlie Dobbs," Fisher exclaimed loudly. "Dobbs would just as soon kill you as look at you. You could be one day old or ninety years old, he'd kill you if he thought you blinked wrong. He's sadistic and evil, but a pro."

"How do you know? What proof do you have that it was Moroni and this guy." Bruce said.

"I don't have any goddamn proof! I never have any fucking proof when it comes to these guys," Fisher said angrily, and loudly. "They cover up their tracks by killing. I can't search their house, their cars, their toilet, or a bicycle without a judge giving authorization, and by then it's too late. The fucking law helps the criminal. The law doesn't give a shit about the victims, only the rights of the perpetrator. Isn't that a nice name for an asshole?" He stood and walked around the patio, his drink in one hand.

The couple in the trailer next door looked out their window at them.

Fisher saw them, and lowered his voice. "And, man, the asshole has a book full of rights. If there was a war going on here, I could kill these bastards and no one would say a word. But this is peacetime and we obey the law, what we can and can't do. So, little boys and little girls, wives, and good guys get slaughtered. And who gives a shit? Not the law, that's for sure." He paused and looked directly into his friend's eyes. "But I know it was Moroni and Dobbs!"

"You're asking to take the law into your own hands, Billy, and then who's the criminal?" Bruce said gently. "If all the cops, and there are many asshole cops, too, could investigate all the robbers and killers without the law's guidance, we'd be in a real pickle. A pickle known as anarchy, Billy. Then we would have a mess."

Fisher seemed to relax. He sat, and he chuckled. "Always the teacher. Eh?"

"We do the best we can with what we have," Bruce said. "And you're very good at it, Billy."

"Sure, I killed Homer and his family, that's all. I left him inside too long."

"You know that now," Bruce said. A smile appeared. "I wish I could bet on the horse today that won yesterday. Stop blaming yourself."

"Moroni didn't have to kill Homer," Fisher said. "Homer didn't know that much, and if he had he wouldn't have stayed. Moroni knew that. He's not dumb. And the family? Why Homer's family? What could he have told his wife that we didn't know, which wasn't much. His wife and children didn't know enough about him or his organization to fill the end of a pin."

Fisher reached over and with his forefinger tapped Bruce's left thigh. "The bastard killed them as a warning to others to leave him alone. As a warning to us. As a warning to underworld characters competing for the high and the mighty. 'Leave Moroni alone or this will happen to you.' That's what this was all about, and what an awful price to pay."

"Why do you know it's Moroni?" Bruce said.

"Gang wars or retaliations don't leave their victims like that. It's all over with in a hurry. Rat-a-tat-tat, chain you to death, stab you in the back, or shoot you from a passing car. They don't take the time and gamble to go out on an overpass and hang the body and empty his guts, blood, and penis all over the freeway. Or place dynamite in or around a house. That's the Mafia way. The Costa Nostra. A four member family is dead. That's how they do business. They call it retribution." A cruel smile appeared on Fisher's face. "Gangs don't put the victim's car in your driveway."

"What?" Bruce said.

"Yeah. I go out to my garage this morning, and there's Homer's car in my driveway, like a calling card. The last we knew of the car it was parked on Moroni's estate in Hillsborough."

"That makes it pretty obvious," Bruce said quietly.

"Sure it does, but there's no proof. No evidence to bring the bastards in. The simple reply would be, 'What car?' But they wanted me to know." Fisher paused a few moments. "One other little thing. Why pick the overpass on Millbrae Avenue to hang the body from and dump the guts? You don't think it could be that I live in Millbrae, just a mile away? Do you?"

Bruce nodded. "Yes, it's obvious."

"Yeah, it's obvious. Big deal." Fisher became pensive. He studied his highball glass. "I'm going to resign, Bruce. Washington called and they want me to come there. They want to question me and I'm sure they feel I'm doing a piss poor job. I'm going to beat them to the punch and resign. I fly out tomorrow."

"You're not going to do any such thing," Bruce said. "You've gotten to know Moroni and his family pretty well over the past two years. You know how he works. You're beginning to know how he thinks. The Director will know that. Stick with it, you're needed. A break will materialize. It usually does."

There was a long pause. "Bruce, you're in terrible danger with this woman."

Bruce smiled. "She's not 'this woman', Billy. Kate Stevens is the woman I love. A woman who has brought so much happiness into my life. I can't leave her, or go without seeing her. Would you if you were in my place?"

"No, I guess not," Fisher said. "But, please be careful."

"I'll try. Billy, I don't want Kate to ever know, or even guess, about Homer and his family. She would find some reason to blame herself."

"I understand, she'll never know."

Bruce stood, picked up the glasses, and started to enter the trailer.

Glenn Mathews

"You've been seeing a lot of Kate Stevens. Haven't you?" Fisher said.

Bruce stopped. "Not as much as I'd like. Kate has been visiting her father in San Mateo the last couple days. I was over there two nights ago for dinner. She'll be back in Sonoma tomorrow and I'll be seeing her the next few days before returning to Tiller."

"Then what?"

"Oh, I don't know." Bruce smiled. "I wouldn't be at all surprised if she came for a visit over Thanksgiving. I'm going to ask her to bring her dad, and to ask her son to come. Her daughter in Chicago is welcome to come if she can. Her family can stay overnight in the owner's trailer next door. I hope her children can come, it'll give us a chance to get to know one another."

"Sounds to me like their approval of you is important, and your relationship with Kate is becoming quite serious."

"Yes, you're right. Simply put, we need to be with each other." Bruce opened the trailer door. "Come on, let's go inside. How does steak, corn, mashed potatoes, out of a box, of course, and salad sound?"

Christy cocked her head at Bruce when she heard the word steak.

"Fine, but I'm going to have another drink, or two. And I may even get drunk on you," Fisher said.

"That's okay, too. You can sleep on the couch."

The three of them went into the trailer.

Chapter Eleven

Sonoma, California. December 23, 1991.

A completely decorated seven foot Christmas tree stood in the corner of the family room where the television was normally seen. Gaily wrapped packages were scattered under the tree and on the end of the hearth nearest the tree. A recently ironed silk cloth covered the stand and most of the carpeting under the boughs, its red could be seen between the presents.

The television was moved to the other side of the hutch nearest the dinette and Kate turned it off. She returned to the sofa and sat beside Bruce, her back partially leaning against him. His arms went around her and his hands relaxed on her lap. His lips brushed her right ear. "Do you want to know something?" he said.

"What?"

"I love you very much."

"I love you, my darling." She placed his right hand against her lips and kissed the palm.

His left hand slowly began to separate the folds of her robe and the right hand gently touched the top of her left thigh. He began to explore. "Do you want to know something else?"

"What?"

"You're not wearing any undergarments," he said.

"Do you mind?"

"Not in the least." He chuckled. "And you know that." His hands began to play with the curls of her pubic hair, then the slight protrusion of her stomach. The hand searched the navel and gradually went to the inner thigh gently insisting that she spread her legs.

She opened her legs slightly and his hand found her opening. "What are you doing?" she said.

He laughed softly into her ear. "You've asked me that same question many times, and you know exactly what I'm doing. And you never close your legs. I wonder why?"

"Because I love you so much," she said. "I want you so. All you have to do is touch me, and I just get ready. I think I'm already wet inside." She turned and sat against the sofa.

His arms enveloped her, and they kissed for a long time. They separated but their faces remained close. Their eyes examined each other for several moments. His tongue gently caressed her nose, her cheeks, and then her lips, suddenly insisting that she open her mouth.

Her tongue shot out and he sucked it well into his mouth. His hands began to remove the robe and she helped him. Soon she was naked and her hands became active at his belt and fly. They continued to kiss, their tongues probing.

He stood and quickly removed his clothes. He sat next to her, his left arm went around her and his right hand caressed her breasts. Soon the hand was massaging the crevice to her vagina. A finger began to explore the interior wetness. Then two fingers were inside her. The fingers went in and out several times. The wetness became sticky.

Kate moaned. She reached for his penis and discovered that he was fully erect.

"Take your fingers out," she said.

She was impatient. She straddled him and the penis quickly penetrated the slippery cavern. He felt her loveliness and he wanted more and more of her. She moved up and down on him, her movements becoming quite rapid. His eyes were half closed in ecstasy. He began to move with her, faster and faster, his back and lower shoulders arched off the sofa.

He came with a convulsion of spurts. He sat back on the sofa in complete exhaustion. His eyes were closed but his softness remained inside her. He smiled. "Wham, bam, thank you, ma'm."

"Yes, squirt, squirt, squirt, and it's all over." She laughed softly.

He opened his eyes and the expression was serious. "I'm sorry. I know it didn't last very long, but I wanted you so very much."

"Don't be sorry, please." she said. "You're so very considerate of me, and I love it when you come. I feel so much a woman, then." She kissed him on the tip of his nose, stood, put on her robe, and went to the bathroom.

He went into her bedroom and got his robe. He checked on the Labs, one in each corner of the bedroom in their respective beds. He went upstairs to the bathroom, then returned to the family room and called the dogs. They came scurrying around the corner of the kitchen from the hallway, the black one in front. He opened the door at the rear of the family room and the dogs went through the screen door opening, the black one insistent on being first. Both were back at the door in less than a minute.

Bruce went outside and pointed a finger at the rear yard. "Now, you gals, just go back out there and do your business. You're not getting your nighttime treat until you do what you came out here to do. So, don't pull a fast one on me."

When they came inside Kate was in the kitchen making tea and getting a dessert out of the refrigerator. "These dogs," Bruce said. "All they care about is their treat, and they forget about crapping and peeing." He removed a box from a cupboard and gave each dog a dog biscuit. "Now, go back to bed. That's it for tonight."

"We all like our treats. Don't we dear?" She looked at him and smiled.

"Uh, huh," he said.

They finished their dessert and they sat on a sofa holding hands and enjoyed the tree.

"I wonder what that big blue one is with the white ribbon and bow?" Kate pointed to a present under the tree.

"That's none of your business, and I don't want you lifting it, or shaking it. Do you hear me?" He laughed.

"Yes, o' great master!" She looked at her present again. "You know, you're very good at wrapping presents."

"The best." He paused. "Kate, I'm going to get up early tomorrow morning, around five, and go back to the trailer park in Napa. I have a couple more presents to wrap there, and things to do, and I'll be back here tomorrow for dinner."

"Why can't you wrap the presents here?" She was aware now that he was concerned about something.

"Well, you have to get up and go to work in the morning," he said. "And your children and your father will be here tomorrow afternoon. You should have the opportunity to be with them, alone, without me hanging around all the time."

"You're talking nonsense," she waved her hand. "And I open the shop tomorrow at eleven and close at three. What really is the matter?"

"I don't want to stay overnight with you when your family is here," Bruce said. "It's just not right. We're not married, you know. I'll come and go from Napa over the next few days."

"But it's all right to screw on the sofa and all over the house when no one is here even though we're not married." She was becoming angry, and they no longer held hands.

"That's different, we're alone, and we have our privacy."

"And it's all right to screw in your home, your trailer, over Thanksgiving when Dad and Eddie are next door."

"Yes, they were not in my trailer, and there was a yard between us," Bruce said.

"You're a hypocrite," Kate exclaimed. She got off the sofa and walked back and forth in front of the fireplace. "Karen and her boyfriend are staying here overnight in the double bedroom upstairs, and Dad and Eddie will stay in the twin bedroom. There's no reason we can't be together downstairs!"

"I've given you my reason." Bruce sounded angry. "And I never permitted my sons to bring their girlfriends into my home and sleep together. They had to be married. I couldn't prevent them from screwing in a car, in a motel, or in a park, but not in my home if they weren't married."

He got off the sofa, looked at her and talked louder. "But this is your home and if you want your daughter to screw without a license, that's your business. Not mine. But a mother should set a good example."

"It's not what I want, but what they want, and what's practical." She almost screamed, coming close to him. "We do live in the nineties."

He turned his back on her. "I get so damn tired of hearing that we live in the nineties. And the morals of this country are going down the tubes," he hollered. He turned around and looked at her. "Do you know what caused the fall of the Roman Empire? And the fall of the Greek Empire? Orgies, that's what. Immoral behavior. Decadence. Soon, it will be the fall of the United States of America!"

The two Labs had entered the family room and were sitting quite close together.

"You and your holier-than-thou-morals," Kate said. "But it's all right to screw me in my home anytime you want to without a license. And you sure like to do it. Don't you? It just depends on who's doing the screwing. That's what." She sat on a sofa, crossed her legs, swinging the top one.

"I guess I know when you don't want me to make love to you anymore. And you don't have to be so vulgar about it," Bruce said.

He looked at the dogs. "And you two go back to bed." He followed them into the bedroom. "I'll get my things together and leave now."

He fussed in the bedroom, not really accomplishing anything. From the closet he got a small cloth suitcase and placed it on the bed. He sat on the bed.

"The future will prove I'm right," he mumbled.

He wondered what she was doing.

He left the bedroom and went toward the family room. She hurried toward him and they were in each other's arms. They kissed passionately, and then their kiss became tender. "I'm sorry," he murmured. "I'm really sorry, darling. I shouldn't have talked to you like that."

"I'm sorry, too, for the same reason," she said quietly. "If you have to stay in Napa I'll try and understand. I do understand."

"I can't help myself," he said. "I'd be very uncomfortable being with you overnight with family in the house." He hesitated. "I just can't help feeling the way I do."

"That's all right, I understand." She hugged him harder. "Let's not talk about it anymore. I want to go to bed with you now. I want you to hold me."

He had his arms around her. Her body pressed against him, wanting his nearness. They were nude, but not passionate.

"I know this will sound corny," he said softly. "Anyway, I would've thought it to be corny at one time. But I mean what I'm going to say." He paused, and took a breath. "Since meeting you, that day in your gift shop, and falling in love with you, I could never live without you. Life wouldn't be the same without you."

She kissed his cheek. "I know," she murmured. She raised her head and looked at him. "But that first day in the shop, you didn't fall in love with me. You wanted to get in my pants. I could tell." She laughed and put her head back on the pillow, close to him.

"Well, I guess so. After seeing you, I wanted in, all right," he said. "But when we went out together I knew I wanted to be with you. And even then I felt a love that I never experienced. I've never known such a complete love. And I never realized that physical love could be so marvelous." He kissed her lightly on the mouth. "You know I love you. Don't you?"

"Oh, yes," she said. "But I think I love you more."

"Impossible."

"Maybe."

"Kate, I want you to know something. I want you to know that I've never felt like this with anyone else before. With you, I'm so, so comfortable. Everything we do is so natural. Whether we make love, eat, talk, in the car, at a movie, whatever, I'm so completely relaxed with you."

"I know. I feel the same way," she said. "And we're relaxed and comfortable with one another because we belong together. It's that simple."

He hugged her and kissed her forehead. "I love you so."

"I love you," she said.

He turned toward a crackling sound in the wall by the ceiling. "What is that?"

"Selma. It's Selma, she's up and about," Kate said.

"Selma? Who the hell is Selma?"

Christy left her basket and the room. She was heard going upstairs.

"Selma is a ghost. A very friendly ghost, but she's sad and restless at times."

"You've got to be kidding."

"No, I'm very serious," Kate said.

Bruce started to laugh. "How do you know she's restless and sad?"

"She told me," Kate said seriously. "Selma was the first occupant in this house. She and her father, a widower. She met a young man at the store and he came to call on her. He visited many times." She turned on her side toward him, raising herself on an elbow. "She was never permitted to go out with him, but they fell in love. When the father was told that they were in love, he ordered the young man out of his house and told him never to return. The father was a selfish man wanting his daughter to wait on him, and not to fall in love. He wanted a free cook and a housekeeper. The young man never returned and Selma died eleven months later. She was only nineteen."

She lay back on the pillow. "They say she had consumption, but she died from a broken heart."

"And she's a ghost here waiting for her man to return," Bruce said sarcastically.

"That's right."

"Uh, huh. Typical," he said. "And she told you all this?"

103

"Yes. She's a sweet thing," Kate said. "I verified everything she told me. I talked to neighbors, older people who are still living."

"And that's where you dreamed up Selma," Bruce said. "From neighbors and your imagination. Sweetheart, you can really fantasize. It's unbelievable."

"I didn't make that noise you heard," Kate said calmly. "And I didn't tell Christy to leave the room and go upstairs. Have you ever known Christy to act like that?"

"No, I haven't," he said frankly.

"Christy and Selma get along fine. They like each other. You've noticed Christy upstairs quite a bit. Haven't you? She goes in the twin bedroom where Selma usually is, the room over this bedroom. Selma called for her a little while ago. She wanted to tell Christy something."

Bruce shook his head slowly. He didn't know how to respond. "And you see her?"

"Yes. Well, I see through her," Kate said matter-of-factly. "Not a lot, but she's tiny, very pretty, shy, and she dresses conservatively."

"Uh, huh. Why don't I see her? Why can't I talk to her?"

"Because you don't believe in her," Kate said.

They heard Christy come into the bedroom. She went to the front window and looked outside. The curtains were parted and she stayed at the window for several minutes. She finally returned to her basket. Sally was sound asleep.

"Make love to me," Kate murmured.

They made love for nearly an hour, and then she was sleepy.

"You'll be here tomorrow afternoon by four," she whispered.

"I will. I have lots to do tomorrow so I'm getting up early, but I won't wake you in the morning. You sleep in. I love you," he said.

"I love you, darling. My wonderful darling." In a few seconds she was asleep.

He stayed awake and thought about Selma.

Sleep finally came.

Bruce was out of bed at four-thirty in the morning.

Christy was wide awake and watched him.

He looked at the dog and placed a forefinger to his lips. He went to the bathroom and took a quick shower.

He got his few things together and placed them in a suitcase. He noticed that Christy kept pacing back and forth. Several times she went into the family room and then came back to the bedroom. She went to the window and looked at the black night, and then she went to the family room again.

Bruce thought she ought to know by now that she was going with him. He attributed her odd behavior to the beginnings of senility.

He had parked the Suburban by the curb in front of the house and he used the side exit off the family room to reach the driveway and take his suitcase and toilet article kit to the truck.

Christy went with him. They walked on the driveway and she kept very close to Bruce's right leg. He almost fell when she pushed her body over his right foot.

"What's the matter with you," he mumbled. "Cut that crap out!"

He reached the truck and placed the suitcase and kit on the floor by the backseat. "Get in," he said quietly to Christy.

They were on the street side of the vehicle. Christy sat on the street. She looked all around and refused to get in the truck. A low growl came from her.

Bruce knew something was wrong with her, but he was just as insistent.

"I said get in the truck, and I mean it!" He tapped her behind with his right foot.

Christy continued to sit, but turned her head to look at her master. She jumped on the backseat.

He returned to the bedroom and picked up the dog basket. When he left the family room he locked the door and walked to the rear of the Suburban. With his key, he lowered the tailgate window and then lowered the tailgate. Christy jumped over the back of the rear seat and was quite close to him. He pushed her gently to the right to make room for the dog basket in the back of the vehicle.

Bruce placed his hands under the tailgate to raise it.

Christy barked sharply and growled viciously.

Bruce knew someone was behind him and he knew he had to duck. Christy flew past his head as a blow landed on the back of his neck.

Bruce felt severe pain and he slumped over the tailgate and gradually slipped to the pavement. He doubled up and moved to his left side as the hard boot hit him in the stomach. Another kick, and another, and his ribs hurt badly. The next kick hit him on the top of the forehead and he could feel the blood dripping over his brows and into his eyes. He knew he was losing consciousness.

Christy's body hit Roy on the top of the chest. She glanced off him and fell to the street. She got up and Roy kicked her in the ribs on her left side. She squealed in pain and lay on the street for several moments watching the man kicking her master. She got up, growled viciously, and grabbed Roy's left pants cuff. She held on to the fabric and moved backward.

Roy tried to kick her with his right leg but he almost lost his balance. He took out his revolver but was unable to aim straight.

Bruce crawled slowly alongside the truck and reached the door on the driver's side. Using the running board, he raised himself to his knees. With difficulty and in pain, he was able to open the door.

Roy reached him, his pants torn to the knee. He kicked Bruce on the small of the back just over his right kidney. Bruce fell against the inside of the open door and dropped to the pavement on his side. Roy moved his right foot back to kick again but Christy got a fresh hold on his pants, on the right leg above the cuff. She pulled hard. Roy was off balance and he fell on the street.

Bruce lifted himself to the floor of the car. He reached under the seat and removed a knife, the blade was five inches long. He had lost most of his breath and he felt faint but he lowered himself to the pavement, his face toward the street side.

Roy got up. The pants had ripped again. He reached down, and working around the dog he awkwardly tore the lower portion of the fabric from his leg. Christy held on as long as she could.

Roy grabbed Bruce's shirt near the collar.

Bruce crooked his left forefinger at him.

Roy raised Bruce closer to his face. The knife entered Roy's belly and he let go of the shirt. His eyes opened wide.

Bruce fell back. Blood was in his eyes and he could hardly see. He saw blurred legs, and hands on a stomach. He lunged and pushed the knife upward. He stabbed Roy's scrotum, the knife went through and entered the underbelly.

Roy screamed. Blood poured from his stomach and down his legs. He staggered, and fell. He got up slowly.

With two hands, Roy held his stomach and crotch and staggered to a car. He got in and started the engine. The car moved slowly down the street.

The screams woke Kate. She put on her robe quickly and ran out the front door of the house and toward the street. Sally ran with her. She got to Bruce just as he collapsed and lost consciousness. She knelt beside him.

A neighbor came out. "What's the matter?" he yelled.

"Dial nine-one-one, and get an ambulance here quick. A man is badly hurt," Kate hollered.

She held Bruce's right hand, a tear ran down her cheek. She looked at Christy. Sally sat beside the black Lab.

Christy lay beside her master.

Roy drove erratically. He got about five miles away and his car went over the right shoulder of the road and into a ditch. The motor was still running when the vehicle came to a stop. Roy's upper torso and head leaned against the steering wheel. The horn blared. The eyes stared blankly at the dashboard.

107

Chapter Twelve

Three days later.

The day had been clear but cold. Twilight began and the outside air was fresh and clean. The hospital bed was raised for Bruce's upper torso to be higher than the rest of his body. He could look out his first floor window at the grass, three trees, and the four bushes that could be seen. Cars lined the curb several yards from the window, and the sidewalk was normally busy during the daylight and early evening hours. The main entrance to the hospital was a half block from Bruce's window.

A nurse came into the room and smiled when she raised the window blind. He was asleep. She gently took his hand. "Mister Campbell," she said. "You have visitors outside waiting to see you."

He was drowsy when he glanced at the hallway door.

"Visitors? Where are they? Have them come in."

"No, sir, you're looking in the wrong direction," she said. "By outside, I mean out there on the grass. Look out the window."

Bruce saw Karen Moroni holding Christy with a taut leash and Eddie Moroni holding another leash on Sally. Both dogs seemed delighted to see him through the window.

Christy's squeal led to a talkative growl and several sharp barks were heard. She pulled the leash and wrapped herself around Karen's legs. She panted with excitement. Sally sat beside Eddie's left leg. Her tail wagged vigorously, and she panted but displayed a big grin.

Bruce laughed and waved.

Christy's barking continued and he placed a finger to his lips. She stopped barking.

In a few minutes the twins disappeared with the dogs. He knew they would be going to the parking lot to put them in the car, and then Kate's children would be coming to his room for a visit.

"What beautiful Labradors," the nurse said. "But I thought that Labs were either black or blond. Why is the one so white?"

"Sally, the white one, is considered a blond Labrador, but white is not uncommon," Bruce said. "However, there's a third color, chocolate."

"Do all these colors of Labradors have the same disposition?" the nurse said.

"They're a gentle breed and highly intelligent. I've never known one to bite, and they're good to children, very patient with them, and generally the Lab is extremely close to one person. But, other than that, and depending on the color, they do display different personalities and characteristics."

"But I was told the black one saved your life."

"That's true," Bruce said, "but I'm sure she didn't bite him. Christy would just worry him to death."

The nurse laughed. She went out the door when the visitors arrived. "He's all yours," she said.

Eddie and Karen Moroni entered the room.

"You look like hell," Eddie said. "And I thought we could go fishing in the morning." He plopped on one of two chairs in the room. His short frame wore gray sweatpants, a blue sweatshirt and blue tennis shoes.

Bruce laughed. "Don't make me laugh. My ribs and stomach hurt." His head was bandaged completely, the wrapping came to the top of his brows and just over his ears.

Karen sat on the bed by his right hand. Her feet could not touch the floor. She wore black baggy slacks, a loose fitting red wool sweater, a forty-niner football cap, and white tennis shoes. She took his right hand and cupped it into her palms. "Mother said you'll be out of here in the morning."

"I guess so," Bruce said. "But I keep this damn head bandage on for a few more days. Then they'll take the stitches out and take another head x-ray. The first one showed a slight fracture but the doctor said the crack will heal on its own, and no damage to the brain."

"Other than what already existed, of course," Eddie said.

Bruce glanced at the young man. He looked at Karen. "Is your brother always like this?"

"Most always, but just don't pay any attention to the asshole." She glared at her brother and stuck her tongue out at him. "Mother's coming again this evening, and she's worried that you're going to say no. But you really have no choice, and that's that."

"No, about what?"

"Where you're going to sleep when you leave here tomorrow," Karen said. "You're staying downstairs in Mom's bedroom, and that's final." She got off the bed and sat on a chair near Bruce. "Mom and I will stay in the double bedroom, Eddie and your son, Steve, in the twin bedroom, and granddad will sleep on the couch. David and his family will stay at a Best Western just four blocks away. By the way, we're anxious to meet your family."

"Granddad will love sleeping on a couch. An old man like that will look forward to sleeping on a couch especially when he comes all the way from San Mateo to get some rest," Eddie said sarcastically. "And we want you to worry about his sleeping on a couch particularly when you're in such great condition and have nothing else to worry about."

"What about Richard, your boyfriend? Where is he staying?" Bruce said.

"Richard left this morning for Libertyville, in Illinois. He made plans to spend the last part of his holiday vacation with his parents," Karen said.

"And we're all going to have our Christmas tomorrow night. Presents have not been opened except for Richard's gifts. We're doing this just so you can be with us. Isn't that sweet?" Eddie pantomimed playing a violin.

"I've certainly been a problem," Bruce said.

"No problem," Karen said. "And, anyway, these plans give Eddie and me the opportunity to meet your sons and David's family, and we can all spend our Christmas together."

"And you had no control over what happened to you," Eddie said. He clenched his fists. He stood and paced in front of the bed. "We have to do something to try and make things easier for you. We care about you, you know, and not just because our crazy father put you where you are. He's caused all your pain. He planned this to happen at Christmastime. That's his gift to Mother."

Bruce saw the young man's anger and hate. "You two can't be responsible for what your father does, or did. And you both are more aware of that fact than I am." He paused and glanced from one to the other. "I have to tell you kids something, and I'm grateful that we're together now." He paused again. "I may have to go after your father. I have a feeling this situation isn't going to end here. If that's the case, I'll retaliate. I may--"

"Kill the son of a bitch!" Eddie nearly screamed. "He's an evil crazy son of a bitch that's no good to anyone. One day he'll hurt or kill Mother. I can feel it."

Bruce observed Karen. There were tears in her eyes but she nodded her head slowly. "Yes, if you have to. But Father is awfully strong. He has access to professionals, and you're --"

"Too old?" Bruce smiled.

"Not too old for Mom. That's for sure," she said, a sparkle now in her eyes. "But you're only one person, and Father has an empire." She stood and went to the bed.

"One person with an older dog. According to scientific statistics Christy is about seventy-seven years old. And she's still full of vigor. She did all right. Didn't she?" Bruce tried to sound cheerful but he wasn't effective. He became serious, and he patted her hand. "Don't you worry about me, Karen, I'll be okay." He saw her tears. "Don't worry, I'll be all right."

He changed the subject. "When are you two going to get my sons? And I understand my grandson and Jan are coming, too. Jesus, you'd think I was being buried."

"No, just being loved," Karen said. She turned to her brother. "When do we pick them up?"

Eddie glanced at his watch. "In about two hours at the Oakland Airport. It'll take us awhile to get there, and we have to take the dogs back to the house. We better go."

"Take George, there will be six of you and the luggage, you'll have more room," Bruce said. "There should be keys by the calendar in the kitchen."

"Thanks, I'll do that," Eddie said. "Come on, sis."

"Before you go there's something I want you both to promise," Bruce said. "Your mother and I discussed the problem earlier this morning and she agreed." He waited for a moment, casually inspecting each of them. His eyes were sober. "Don't ever tell my sons or Dave's wife the real cause for my being here. They don't need to know about Moroni. Just tell them it was a mugging. Some guy tried to rob me, Christy and I fended him off. That's what was in the paper."

"How can they believe that when the police tied in your assailant with the Filipino found stabbed to death in his car on the side of the road?" Eddie said. "The blood in the car matched the blood in the street, and your general description makes it complete."

"So, I killed my assailant. So what?"

"And this same Filipino was identified as Roy Machato who just happens to work for our father," Karen said. "His picture was in the paper, you know. And your family will know our last name."

"I doubt very much that this Roy will ever be associated with Mafia," Bruce said. "Your father is too smart for that to happen. His employment will be hushed up. If he is, I'll tell my boys then. But I'd rather not, and only if I have to." He had a guilt look, but he was adamant. "Dave, in particular, is a terrible worrywart. He'd worry himself sick about me if he knew the truth, and there's nothing he can do about it. He has a lot of important responsibilities to be concerned about."

"And it's very important to you that your sons like Mom, and not hold a grudge against her," Eddie said.

"And to like us and not know we're the children of the man that's caused so much trouble and grief," Karen said.

"Yes, I guess so," Bruce said angrily. "Goddamn it, you kids and your mother can't help what's happened. We're dealing with a fucking maniac. Let's not add to the problem. I'm sorry, Karen, I shouldn't have been vulgar."

"Don't be sorry for telling the truth." She turned and walked a few steps. "Okay, I agree, but they're going to know about the blood, Christy, the struggle, and the fact you killed this guy. It's all in the paper."

"That's all right, but they don't need to know about your father, and what he might still do."

"We'll tell them it was a mugging. I agree," Eddie said. "And I'll make you and Christy to be the heroes of heroes."

"I bet you will, too," Bruce said. "You can really bullshit. Now, you two, get out of here."

Eddie squeezed the blanket over Bruce's right ankle. Karen kissed him on the cheek.

Bruce smiled. "You know," he said quietly, "I don't have any ill feelings toward Richard. I was pleased that he came to see me. He's a nice young man. But I wish my son, Steven, had met you sooner, and you two had the opportunity to know one another."

"Who knows?" Karen said. "Richard and I just agreed to delay our marriage. We seem to keep doing that. And I'm meeting your younger son in a couple of hours." There was mischief in her eyes, and she blinked them twice at him. "Bye-bye."

Kate visited an hour later. She placed a hand behind the bandaged head and kissed him softly on the lips. She sat on a chair. "How are you feeling?"

"Hurt some in the ribs and gut, but the doctor said this afternoon that the pain will eventually go away," Bruce said. His eyes examined her and he liked what she had on. She wore a red cashmere sweater with black cotton slacks. She had removed the red wool knee length coat.

"Have they examined your heart?"

"Yes, everything's fine. Stop worrying," he said. "I guess they don't tape cracked ribs anymore. They heal on their own, but they do give me stiff doses of ibuprofen for the pain and it helps. I'll have a prescription of it when I leave. The back feels better with it, too. I'm going to be fine, sweetheart."

"That's what the vet said too about Christy," Kate said sadly. "When that lump appeared on her side I got scared. He said a kick probably caused it and that the swelling is just fluid and it will dissipate, and that the ribs will heal also on their own."

She lowered her head and cupped a hand over her brow. She cried softly.

"What's the matter?" he said tenderly.

"Oh, what is he going to do next? He won't stop as long as we continue to see each other."

"That's his excuse now. What do you want to do about us? Do you want us to say goodbye? To part? To never see each other again? To obey his wishes?" He was angry.

"No," she said quietly. "I could never be without you. I love you very much."

"I love you," he said softly, the anger gone. "Let's not ever again talk about what he's going to do next, or that we should part. We'll deal with anything that may come as long as we're together."

She nodded.

"I really like your children. They have a way about them that makes you feel good," Bruce said.

"They like you, darling. They feel comfortable with you. Eddie idolizes you." She was smiling now. "He had a wonderful time over Thanksgiving. The laughter, the steelhead fishing, the games we played. And Dad had a ball, too. Eddie needed a father. And although Karen has only known you a couple days, she really is fond of you. I know."

"I'm glad." There was shyness on his face.

She had a worried look. "I'm kind of jittery. I want very much for your sons to like me, and David's wife and son. I hope all goes well." She looked at him lovingly.

"Now listen to me," Bruce said. "All of them will like you. Don't fret. Just be yourself. Dave and Steve want me to be happy. I know that. And they know how happy I am with you. We've talked a lot about you and me on the phone." He smiled at her. "And I don't need to be in the picture, they can't help but like you." He raised the bed a little higher, the back felt more comfortable. "And I think you will like all of them."

"I know I will," she said. "And I will give you a full report." She laughed.

He seemed embarrassed and disturbed about something.

"You know, well, eh. About that thing upstairs in the --"
"Selma?"

"Yeah," he nodded. "Well, you know, I got to thinking. I know this is all nonsense and ridiculous, but I got to thinking that she must have told Christy something when she called her upstairs. Something about someone being outside on the street. Waiting for me. Do you remember Christy coming down and going to the window in your bedroom and looking outside for a longtime?"

"Yes, I remember," Kate said matter-of-factly.

He felt foolish despite being serious.

"Yeah. Well--, when we went outside to get things in George, Christy was being protective of me. She kept looking around, getting in my way, and not wanting to get into George. And she was ready for something. So, I thought --"

"You want me to thank Selma for saving your lives." Kate smiled.

"Well I don't know that I'd go to that extreme." He hesitated. "If you happen to see Selma you might just tell her that I thank her, and wish her well."

"I'll just do that. But you know, sweetheart, you're beginning to believe in--, in another type of soul. You just might

Glenn Mathews

be able to thank her yourself." Kate had a gentle smile on her face.

The visiting hours had been over for an hour but the hospital staff didn't argue with William Fisher. Fisher displayed credentials and he was escorted to the patient's room.

Bruce dozed. A book was still on his lap and a light shone by the bed. He felt a presence. He opened his sleepy eyes. "I was wondering when you were going to show up."

Fisher sat on a chair. "That bastard worked for Moroni. There's no question of it."

"Good, now we're getting somewhere. What's your proof?"

"You keep asking me that. I have no proof, Goddamn it!" Fisher exclaimed. "I had an agent question Moroni. Sure, he had a Roy working for him. He didn't recognize a picture shown to him, did not know a Machato. And had no pictures of the Roy who worked for him, and had recently left."

"Surely Homer had to make written reports to you. This Roy's name had to be mentioned," Bruce said.

"Oh, Homer made reports, alright. And Roy, the Filipino, was mentioned. Homer told us he worked for Moroni as a valet and bodyguard," Fisher said. "How many Filipinos named Roy are there in this country? Homer's not around to identify him. He didn't give us a last name. His surname Machato doesn't help now. Do you think Moroni gave him a payroll check made out to Roy Machato, got his social security number and deducted for unemployment and social security benefits? That'll be the day," Fisher said caustically.

He stood and went to the window. "Roy was paid with cash. A Roy paid with cash, just like Homer, only paid to Smitty. We even talked to the woman Roy shacked up with in San Francisco. We got an address and surname off his driver's license. She was scared to death. She said that her Roy was currently unemployed, didn't know what he was doing in the wine country. She said he had worked as a valet, and had a job at one time in

116

the garment business. She knew he always had cash but she never knew where it came from. She was lying, but she would have died rather than tell us the truth. The car wasn't much help either. It was a rental."

Bruce was disappointed. "We're getting nowhere."

"At least you killed the bastard. One less asshole."

"Why not try questioning again that fellow who took Kate out a couple of years ago. The pharmacist," Bruce said. "He can identify Charlie Dobbs. Keep on him, Billy. He's your best bet."

"He moved to San Jose. I sent two agents to visit him right after the murders of Homer and his family." Fisher turned and went to the side of the bed. "He disappeared within hours of those murders and has never been seen since. A witness in a parking lot near the drugstore saw a man resembling the druggist enter a car with another man. Vague description. The witness felt there was no friendship between them. This abduction took place a few hours after Homer's body was hanged from the overpass. The pharmacist is dead, Bruce. God knows where he's buried. He was going to be married soon. A lovely woman. She couldn't help us."

Bruce shook his head slowly. "How many lives has this man affected? All so tragically."

He brightened a bit. "The police were here two days ago. They questioned me for about a half hour, and then left. They said 'thank you'. Everything was very informal. I think you had something to do with that, Billy."

"I might have. There's no reason to get on you. Play the hero." Fisher chuckled. "Damn, I wish I could order a drink."

"I can get you some coffee."

"Thank you, no. Are you feeling better?"

"Oh, I'm fine."

"Yeah, sure. You're aching all over, but you're fine." Fisher looked at his friend for several moments. "He'll be coming for you. Now that his Roy is dead he'll be meaner than shit."

"Let him be mean. He'll make a mistake then."

"Uh, huh. I hope you're right," Fisher said. "But I don't think so."

Moroni sat near his fireplace in the bedroom. He wore white silk pajamas under a black smoking jacket. The massive cement logs looked artificial despite a fire playing around them in methodical boredom.

Charlie Dobbs was permitted to sit on a large chair near him. He wore khaki slacks and a light brown sport's shirt open at the collar.

"You convinced the broad?"

"Yes, Mister Moroni," Dobbs said. "She's not going to say anything other than what I told her to say. I slapped her around a little but I used gloves. She's real frightened."

"Yes, and we don't want to put her away unless we have to. Out of respect to Roy we will leave her alone. Did you give her the money?" the old man said.

"Yes, Mister Moroni. I told her she wouldn't live long enough to spend it if she got us in trouble with the police or those intelligence agents. She'll behave."

"Good. Very good, Charlie. You did well."

"Thank you, Mister Moroni."

The old man became thoughtful. For several minutes he stared at the fireplace.

"Yes, yes, those intelligence agents. Mister Bruce Campbell was one of those agents. You found that out. Didn't you?"

"Yes, sir. He was with the U.S. Army Counter Intelligence Corps during the Korean War."

"Campbell was with this Fisher the night Smitty was there?" the old man said.

"Yes, Mister Moroni, and Fisher went to see Campbell at a trailer park in Napa right after Smitty's death. They had dinner in the trailer. Seems like they're good friends."

"This FBI man and his group are getting tiresome. Obviously, they want information on us."

"That's right, Mister Moroni."

"And Campbell is the one who killed our Roy. Isn't he?"

"Yes, sir, that's what the paper said," Dobbs nodded. "But Roy left his marks on him. The guy is in a Sonoma hospital."

"And Campbell was fucking her?"

"Yes, sir."

"And Campbell is still fucking her?"

"He was before Roy attacked him. All the time," Dobbs said. "When he gets out of the hospital he'll get in her again,-- if you'll pardon the expression, Mister Moroni."

"Yes, I am sure you are right, but we will see." There was a long silence.

"The woman will not learn." The old man's eyes looked furious and hateful. "A wanton woman. She will learn. She will learn. Or, or severe action will be necessary."

An interminable stillness prevailed. The old man had closed his eyes. Dobbs waited. Several minutes elapsed. Dobbs quietly raised himself from the chair.

"Sit down!" the old man said harshly. Dobbs sat. "Didn't you tell me that her father is friendly with this man?" Moroni's voice was pleasant. "I believe you said they fished together in Oregon."

"That's right, Mister Moroni, over the Thanksgiving holiday. She was there, too. And your son was there."

"I have no son, Charlie. Are you referring to Edward?"

"Yes, sir. They were all very, very friendly. If you will excuse me, Mister Moroni, I had the impression that Edward looked upon this Campbell like he was his father."

"His father, eh?" The old man mused. "Yes, yes, a father is very important." He became pensive. "We will wait awhile. To react immediately might be a little obvious, and I have other business to attend to. You may go, Charlie."

Dobbs stood. "Yes, Mister Moroni." He left the room.

The old man folded his hands on his lap. He gazed at the fireplace. An evil smile appeared on his face. "Yes, yes," he whispered. "I think that will do very nicely."

Chapter Thirteen

Three months had quickly passed since Bruce left the hospital. With moderate exercise initially which increased gradually, his condition improved rapidly. The back pain was gone and the ribs no longer ached. His head fracture healed and the scar from the injury and stitches was hardly noticeable. When working in the yard he discovered that he could do more. He could breathe with less difficulty and his arms and legs were stronger.

Rain fell frequently in Oregon despite Bruce's praise for his locality and the repeated assurance that he lived in the 'banana belt'. But by mid-March twenty inches of rain had fallen since the first of the year. Bruce continually watched the river, fearful that the waters would never stop rising, and aware of the old water marks over the doorway of the shed behind the trailer's parking pad. The gentle, shallow and appealing waters seen during late spring, summer and early fall were no longer evident. The creek and river were angry, their torrents swift and deadly, the whitecaps cold and uninviting.

During this time, Bruce and Christy visited Kate and Sally on two separate occasions for a week in Sonoma. Twice, they met in Redding, California, and each time they stayed for three nights at the Red Lion Inn. Redding was halfway between Tiller and Sonoma, and the inn accepted dogs. They visited many interesting places. They had good times together. And they made love.

Stanley Stevens was pleased that he had found a hybrid tea that was so different in color, pure gold. The rosebush was called "Midas Touch' and the name was surely appropriate. Kate will love it, he thought. She always liked the single rose on its long stem, the hybrid tea variety. Kate's birthday was next week and he wanted to please her and to give her what she wanted.

He removed the rosebush from the nursery container and repotted the bush. He added a little fertilizer and watered Kate's new rose. All he needed now was a birthday card. Tomorrow he would work most of the day in the yard. He had lots to do, and already spring was three weeks old.

He entered the kitchen from the backdoor. The coffee maker was kept warm and he poured himself a cup of coffee, added a little milk from the refrigerator, and a teaspoon of sugar from the bowl on the breakfast table in the kitchen nook. He took two swallows.

"Enjoy that, Pop, it'll be the last you'll be tasting for awhile," Charlie Dobbs said.

Stanley froze in terror. He knew the voice. His legs began to tremble. He was afraid to turn around.

"What's the matter, Pop? Aren't you going to say hello? I haven't seen you for sometime. You always were a dip shit." Dobbs stood by the doorway to the dining room.

Stanley turned slowly and suddenly rushed for a drawer. He opened it and grabbed a knife handle. The drawer was kicked shut on his wrist. A blow landed on his left jaw. He slumped over the Formica counter. Stanley knew his jaw was broken. Another blow landed and the pain was more than he could bear. Another blow on the face and he slipped to the floor. Blood oozed from his mouth. Stanley saw and heard nothing.

Dobbs closed the blinds in the kitchen. He went into the dining room and the living room to close the drapes. He picked up the suitcase he left in the living room, returned to the kitchen, walked over Stanley, and placed the bag on the kitchen table. He glanced at the wall clock. The time was six p.m.

"Shit, I got a lot of time to kill," he mumbled.

He took off the leather gloves and put them in the suitcase and pulled a thin pair of latex gloves over his hands. He removed three pieces of rope from the suitcase. Stanley was a small man and there was no problem picking him up and placing him on a kitchen chair. Dobbs tied Stanley's hands behind the chair and his ankles were tied together. A larger piece of rope was wrapped over Stanley's stomach and around the back of the chair twice and tied securely. Stanley's head was lifted and duct tape was placed over the mouth.

"Now let's see what he's got to eat." Dobbs opened the refrigerator and scanned the interior. He removed the T-bone steak that was on a plate. He found a variety of salad ingredients in the bottom drawer.

"Damn, he's even got my favorite dressing, ranch!"

He took a package of shoestring potatoes from the freezer. He discovered two frying pans, searched and found cooking oil, and seasoning. Within minutes the steak and fries were spattering and popping in the pans. He made himself a large green salad and poured a goodly amount of the dressing over it. He noticed Stanley begin to open his eyes. He set a place for himself on the table and poured a large glass of milk. The food was ready and the steak and fries were placed on a dinner plate. He sat to enjoy the meal.

Stanley looked at him. Blood had clotted under his chin. He was terrified. He knew he was going to die. He didn't know the when or where of his death or how he was going to die but he knew death was near and the end would not be nice. He always thought of death as something everyone had to deal with, and when his time came he thought he would welcome it knowing that he would soon be with his wife. He never thought it was going to be like this.

"Pop," Dobbs said with his mouth full. "You shouldn't have gone for that butcher knife. I got to respect you for it, but you didn't have a prayer."

Dobbs cut off a large piece of meat with a steak knife, picked up the piece with his fingers and put the meat in his mouth. The fingers reached for a handful of potatoes and he stuffed his mouth. "Otherwise, no need to hit you. I would've tied you to the chair but your mouth and hands would've been free, and I would've cooked you a meal." He paused.

"Yeah, your last meal before the execution." Dobbs laughed, food spat from his mouth. "And we would've had a nice little talk, too." He laughed. "Now I got to eat all by myself. See what you did."

Stanley closed his eyes. A tear flowed down his face.

"I parked an older Chevrolet sedan in your garage, Pop. I didn't want neighbors seeing a strange car out front and taking a license number."

Dobbs finished the meal and opened the suitcase next to him on the table. He took off the sweaty latex gloves, wiped his hands with a napkin, and put on a fresh pair of gloves. He went to the living room and turned on the television. He searched for a good program and saw that a western movie was about to begin. He hurried into the kitchen and dragged the chair with Stanley into the living room next to a large lounging chair with an ottoman that faced the television.

Dobbs sat, raised his feet, and got comfortable.

Dobbs watched two and a half movies. He fell asleep.

Stanley saw his eyelids flutter and close. He began to move his toes up and down. He had no feeling in his feet and he didn't want to try and move them. Up and down, up and down. Despite being tied around the ankles he felt his feet could move a little. Just a little was all he needed if he could move them.

Dobbs' eyelids remained closed. There was no give to the rope around his hands in back of the chair, but the rope around his stomach wasn't too tight. He could feel his toes.

He began to move his feet from one side to the other. He felt the rope on his feet now. That was good, he thought, the feeling was back. Dobbs still looked asleep.

Very slowly, Stanley stood. He couldn't stand very high and his short height didn't help. The chair felt like a mountain behind him. A low crouch was all that he could achieve. He looked again. Dobbs was still asleep.

He moved his right foot a half inch backward. The left foot joined the right. He continued to move backward until he was out of Dobbs' line of sight. He made it to the dining room and sat down. He breathed heavily, his back hurt, and he was tired. He sat for only a few seconds.

He bent over again and slowly moved backwards. The chair legs on his left rear hit the kitchen door frame. The noise sounded like thunder to Stanley. He looked at the back of the lounge chair. Dobbs' right arm on the armrest hadn't moved. He backed into the kitchen, and he sat again. He arrived at the knife drawer. The fingers on his right hand felt the lower edge of the drawer against the panel.

With fingertips, nails, and knuckles, he was able to open the drawer enough to get a portion of his fingers behind the lip, and he pulled the drawer open. He was able to feel and find his favorite small cutting knife. He was able to cut the rope in back of the chair that went around his stomach and he could move more freely.

He worked on the rope around his wrists. He could feel the pain of a cut and some blood. The fingers kept working and he was determined not to drop the knife. There was a little give and some movement in his hands. He kept working and working the knife until he cut through. He cut the rope around his feet. He ripped off the duct tape from his mouth. He put the small knife on the counter and grabbed the butcher knife.

He ran to the lounge chair. He raised the knife high and moved to the front of the chair. The knife began its plunge. The chair was empty.

"My God, where is he?" Stanley said.

Dobbs tapped his shoulder.

"Are you looking for me?" Dobbs said from behind him. He laughed.

Stanley turned around and raised the knife high.

Like a snake striking, Dobbs grabbed both wrists and squeezed hard. The knife fell out of Stanley's hand. He raised the little man off his feet. Dobbs laughed hard.

"I was peeking at you all the time," Dobbs said. "Feisty little bastard. That was fun!" He guffawed. "And you saved me the trouble of taking all the rope off of you. It's time to go, Pop."

His feet off the ground, Stanley tried to kick him, but he couldn't reach him.

Dobbs lowered him, and he let go of Stanley's left wrist. Dobbs' arm moved backward with a closed fist and he brought it forward quickly. He hit Stanley's already broken jaw. The little man lost consciousness.

Dobbs drove Moroni's sedan to Sonoma. He was on several residential streets until the destination came within sight. He put the car in neutral, cut the motor, shut off the headlights, and the vehicle came to a quiet stop in front of Kathryn Steven's home. A large oak tree was in her front yard.

Dobbs put on a fresh pair of latex gloves and got out of the car. He opened the backdoor and retrieved a long heavy rope with a hangman's noose at one end. He opened the trunk and looked at Stanley. His eyes were open. His mouth was taped. Stanley's hands were tied in front of him.

Dobbs placed the noose around the little man's neck.

"End of the line, Pop," he whispered. "Your daughter has to be taught a lesson, and you're the lesson. A crazy old fart is the teacher. What the hell, I get paid. It's a job." He carried him to the brick pathway nearest the oak tree.

Dobbs placed him on the pathway. He tossed the end of the rope over a heavy branch. He pulled on the rope, hand over hand, and Stanley was forced to his feet. The noose tugged brutally on his neck. The noose became tighter and Stanley was lifted off his feet under the branch.

"I'm coming, my dear ... Goodbye, Kate ... I love ... Oh, I, can't bre ... I'm chok ... I, can't ..."

Dobbs held the rope tightly. The body and legs jerked for several moments, and then they were still. He tied the end of the rope to the trunk of a smaller tree across the pathway from the oak tree. Stanley's feet were eighteen inches above the ground. There was a moderate breeze. The body swayed slightly.

Dobbs drove to a parking lot at a Safeway store not far from Stanley's home in San Mateo. The store was always open. He parked the sedan among the few cars that were there. He looked at his watch. The time was 4:05 a.m. He got out of the car and put the suitcase in the trunk of the Chevrolet. He strolled to a pay telephone near the store's entrance. He dialed a number and was asked to deposit sixty-five cents. He deposited the change.

The phone rang three times. "Hello," Kate answered.

"Open your front door and look outside, Mrs. Moroni." Dobbs hung up and replaced the receiver. He left the phone booth and strolled toward the Chevrolet.

Kate ran and swung the front door open. She turned on the porch light. She saw a little man hanging from a tree.

"Oh, my God. My God. No, no, no. Don't let it be." She ran to the feet and looked up to the anguished face. "Oh, my God. Daddy. Daddy!"

She looked all around. She ran into the house and into the kitchen. She got a knife and ran outside to the smaller tree. She cut and hacked at the rope.

"Hurry, hurry. Goddamn it, hurry!" She cut through, and she heard the body hit the ground.

She turned and ran to her father. She sat beside him and brought his head and shoulders into her arms.

"Daddy, daddy, did I hurt you?" She ripped the tape off his mouth. She looked at his face. "Oh, dear God. No, no, no. No. Daddy. Daddy!"

Her screams could be heard throughout the neighborhood.

Chapter Fourteen

Four days later.

The service was brief and held in the cemetery chapel. Nearly a hundred people came to Stanley Stevens' funeral and after the service they stood outside by the grave site. Stanley was buried next to his wife in a cemetery off Skyline Boulevard between San Mateo and Half Moon Bay in the Bay Area. A light rain fell. Umbrellas were out but no one was really wet or uncomfortable because the weather was mild, and the western horizon showed the promise of clearing. A green canvas covering on four posts with a gable roof was over the casket. There were many flowers. An attractive spray of roses was on top of the casket. A note pinned to one of the stems read, 'We will always love you'. Kate, Karen, and Edward had each signed at the bottom.

A row of four chairs was alongside the casket. Kate's children sat with her and she wanted Bruce to be with them. David and Steven, Bruce's sons, stood nearby.

Dave was thirty-one, five foot ten, 170 pounds, and he had a full head of dark brown hair parted on the left side. Hazel eyes that dominated his face were under thick eyebrows. He had a big nose, full cheeks, and a square chin.

Steve was tall and thin. He had a shallow chiseled face and blond wavy hair that had no part. He was six years younger than his brother, two inches taller, and twenty-five pounds lighter.

The minister recited two prayers. When he had finished he paused a few moments.

"This concludes the service," he said. "Ms. Stevens has asked me to invite all of you to her home in Sonoma. A buffet will be served and she would welcome your friendship. For those wanting information on how to get to Ms. Stevens' home, please ask me, or those two young men over there." He nodded to David and Steven who raised their hands. "Maps are available. Thank you, and God bless you all."

Kate stood and she was escorted to a limousine by Karen and Edward. She was weak and a little unstable on her feet. There were no tears now, only sadness and exhaustion on her face. She was very grateful for her children but she wanted to be with Bruce. She looked behind and saw him standing with his sons and the minister near the casket. She liked his sons. A sad smile appeared. She knew Bruce would stay while they lowered the casket.

The last map was given to a departing mourner. Bruce nodded to the minister. A funeral director saw the gesture and an electric mechanism was activated to lower the casket.

"What now?" David said.

"The top half of a vault will be glued and placed over the casket, and then dirt will be shoveled into the cavity," Steve replied.

"Is that so? I never would have guessed that, smart ass," David said. "How do you know there's a vault?"

"I see the top partially visible under that artificial grass over there."

"Where's the bottom?" David said. "Never mind, it's under the casket."

"That's correct."

"When I go, I won't need any vault," David said.

"Some cemeteries require them, and most families don't want bugs and moisture getting to the departed."

"How do you know all this crap? I thought business and economics were your only interests."

"I do read other subjects, David, always a good policy to be informed. I recommend it."

"You recommend it? Look --"

"Will you two stop," Bruce interrupted. He smiled. "Let's get out of here."

They walked toward Kate's limousine.

"I want you both to go with Kate to her home," Bruce said. "I'll be along in a little while. There's somebody here I want to see."

"It's the guy over there leaning against the car. He sure dresses well," David said.

"He must be the CIA man you trained earlier in your career," Steve said. "Now he's with the FBI."

"You're both right," their father admitted.

"We have to talk to you," David said.

"Very important that we do," Steve said.

"We'll talk, later this evening, when the guests have departed. I promise," Bruce said.

When they arrived Karen opened the backdoor from inside the long Cadillac. Kate sat between her children.

Bruce went inside the car and sat on a jump seat. He took Kate's hand in his, leaned forward and kissed her softly on the lips. "There's someone here that I have to talk to. I'll only be a short time. You go on now."

"How will you get to Sonoma?" Kate said.

"He's a friend. He'll take me. I won't be far behind you." Bruce kissed her again and left. He watched the limousine leave the cemetery. David and Steven sat next to the chauffeur.

A Lincoln took the parking space that was vacated. William Fisher rolled down the window. "Need a ride?"

"Yes." Bruce sat on the passenger side. The rain had stopped, and the car door was left open. "Turn off the ignition, Billy. Let's sit here for awhile."

"All right."

Bruce looked toward the grave site. The grave diggers stamped the ground with shovels. One man dropped his tool and began to replace the grass that had been removed.

"You know," Bruce said. "That little man buried over there never harmed anybody. He wouldn't know how. He loved his wife, his daughter, and his grandchildren. He loved roses, and he had a few friends. I was fortunate enough to be one of them. He enjoyed the little things in life. You never had to make a big to do to please him." Tears were in Bruce's eyes, and one fell down his cheek. "See, Billy, we can all cry at times."

"What can I say, my friend?"

"I guess one could say that I killed him," Bruce said. "I walked into a gift shop not too long ago and I met his daughter. We went out together and we fell in love. I signed his death warrant."

"That's not true."

"Yes, it's true, two plus two equals four."

"Not that kind of truth," Fisher said. "In a world for the insane, yes. We're not dealing with sanity. Your reaction to Kathryn Stevens Moroni was very normal. Hell, if I had known she was unattached and in that gift shop, I would have bought out the store to have her go out with me. It's a damn good thing for you I didn't see her first."

"You knew she was there. You questioned her." Bruce smiled.

"I know. What the hell, I should have gone back."

"Billy, I need a favor."

"I'm afraid to ask."

"I need to know Moroni's schedules. What he does with regularity."

"Stay away from him. I'll get him, eventually. You don't have a prayer!"

"You're probably right, but that's immaterial."

"What happened to all that anarchy talk. You're the one that said not to take the law into your own hands. Remember?"

"I remember."

There was a long pause.

"I'm sorry," Fisher said. "I shouldn't have said that. That wasn't fair."

"Yes, it was. I just don't practice what I preach."

"You're that sure it was Moroni?" Fisher said.

"Who else?"

"I know, I know, Charlie Dobbs' work written all over it. But, as you've always questioned, where's the --"

130

"Proof? There's proof this time, Billy. Kate answered the phone at four o'clock that morning. The voice told her to look out the front door, and referred to her as Mrs. Moroni. Kate recognized the voice of Charlie Dobbs."

"She did?"

"Kate would never testify to that, and I don't blame her. And I would never admit to anyone what I just told you," Bruce said.

"And that's the problem. Somebody has to testify or we'll never get these bastards."

"No one is going to testify if the safety of loved ones is threatened."

"And that's Moroni's greatest asset. Fear. Goddamn fear."

"Did you know that tomorrow is Kate's birthday?"

"No, but it figures."

"Listen to me, Billy." They looked at each other. "I've got to try and stop him. He'll go on like this. Moroni will keep killing. Who'll be next? Me? You? Kate? One of his children? Or, both? My sons? Or someone else? And he has to pay for what he's done. I've got to try. Do you understand me?"

Fisher took a deep breath. He looked away toward the workers at the grave site. They placed flowers.

"I understand," he said quietly. "I'll do what I can. I have the feeling though that I'll be going to your funeral next."

"Maybe."

Forty-one of the mourners had arrived for the buffet and they had departed by early evening. Kate was appreciative of their visit but relieved when they were gone. All four children had kept an eye on Kate during the gathering, wanting to make sure that she was alright. But she handled herself well, and even ate some of the food.

The subjects were unaware of the scrutiny but Kate, Bruce, and the brothers were aware of the affection between Steven and Karen.

A hand was touched or held briefly, or an arm around the waist and a quick hug, or a light kiss on the cheek from Karen.

The viewers were pleased, David being the only one that was surprised.

When the last guest had left there were just the six of them in the living room.

"I'm going to lie down for awhile," Kate said. "There's lots of food left, so help yourself. And there's cake, and there's ice cream in the freezer." She went to Bruce and kissed his cheek. "I love you," she whispered into his ear.

He smiled at her and then she left the room.

An awkward silence enveloped the room for several moments. Steven and Karen sat on a small couch and held hands. Eddie looked at David, and nodded toward the couple.

"I can tell you didn't know about them," Eddie said.

"No. I sure didn't. Shocking, but acceptable," David said. "I didn't think Steve had it in him. I always thought he'd be too busy making money and no time for a woman."

"Impossible," Eddie said. "Unless you're gay, a man always has time for a good-looking broad. And my sister is a good-looking broad."

"Yes, she is, but you don't know my brother. He's always busy being busy, and has never cared to know the fundamentals of sexual behavior. But he knows about vaults, and glue, and cemetery rules. Just ask him."

"Why? Who gives a shit?" Eddie said.

"You know, Steve, these two dimwits are going to get along very well together. They're from the same mold," Karen said.

"Obviously. They both have diarrhea of the mouth, and neither know the facts," Steve said.

Bruce laughed. He enjoyed the banter.

"What facts?" he said.

"Dad, under the circumstances, we don't feel the time is appropriate to inform --"

"Go ahead," Karen interrupted. "Granddad would approve, and I've already told Mom."

"You have?"

Karen nodded.

"All right." Steve glanced at the brothers. He said to his father, "Karen and I are going to be engaged. I want her to have an engagement ring, and she wants one. Soon, we'll pick one out together."

Bruce hugged them. All the brothers shook hands, and Karen was hugged several times. They talked at the same time. Steve grinned at his father. "Yes, Karen and I are completely compatible, in every way."

David turned to Eddie, "Completely compatible? I don't believe it!"

"In every way?" Eddie stared at Steve. "Did you hurt my sister?"

"How do you answer something like that?" Steve said to Karen.

"Don't, just ignore the asshole!" Karen laughed. She looked at Bruce, and her face softened. She led him by the hand to the large sofa.

Steve followed. They sat together.

Karen became serious. "I told Steve everything, Bruce. All about Father and what he's done. I left nothing out. And, together, we told Dave. I couldn't live a lie. Please understand."

"I do understand, Karen," Bruce said. "You couldn't do anything else. It was wrong of me to ask you not to say anything. My sons must know that Kate and her children can't be responsible for the actions of a madman, even when --"

"We do know that," David interrupted. He came near them. "And we're a little disappointed in you that you wouldn't know that. Kate's ex is a bum, and she married him to help her mother and father. She had to get rid of him, and she did. It's that simple. And Karen and Eddie? They never had a father."

David sat on a chair near them. "I don't understand it." He shook his head slowly. "He's done some terrible things. I can't believe what he had done to Mister Stevens. Terrible. But his children and his ex-wife are good people, Dad, and I'm glad they're a part of my life, and a part of yours."

"That's right, I couldn't have said it better," Steve said.

"Thank you, boys. I'm very glad, and very proud of you," Bruce said with watery eyes.

"We don't want you to go after this guy, Dad, you'll get hurt," David said.

"That's what your talk in the cemetery was about. Wasn't it?" Steve looked at him.

"Yes," Bruce said. "And I'm going after him."

"Less than three years ago you had heart surgery. And a few months ago, you got beat up. You're not up to this," Steve exclaimed.

"I'm alright now," Bruce said with finality.

"Then I'll go with you," David said.

"So will I," Steve said.

"No, you will not." Bruce became angry for a moment, then his tone softened. "Let me do what I have to do. By myself. You both know why you can't get involved. Steve, your career and life are just beginning."

He smiled at Karen. "You now have a responsibility. Dave, you have a wife, a career, and many years ahead of you, and a little guy that needs a father. But, most of all, I have to do this alone." He paused and looked at each one of them. "Sometimes in life you have to do something that you really don't want to do, but it needs doing. You know that your life is in danger but you must have the grit to do it. Loved ones are going to worry about you but you can't help yourself and, deep down, they understand. For most, going to war is a good example. Now, I have to go after Moroni. I have to try. And I have to go by myself."

He smiled at them again. "But Christy will be with me."

In the hallway, off the living room, Kate had heard him, and she was crying softly.

A few moments before Bruce left for Napa, Kate came out of the bedroom carrying a small suitcase.

"You kids watch the house," she said. "I'm staying overnight with Bruce in Napa. Sally's coming, too." She opened the door off the family room and the dogs rushed outside and went to the

Suburban on the driveway. They whined to get inside the vehicle.

Bruce seemed surprised for a second.

"Goodbye all," he said. "See you in the morning."

The children went out to the truck with them.

Bruce got behind the wheel, Kate sat beside him. He got out of the truck and went around to the other side. "Son," he whispered to Steve. "This is Kate's home and--, I'd rather you didn't. I'd prefer that you sleep --"

Eddie overheard and interrupted.

"Have no fear, he will not touch my sister. There will be no hanky-panky. Just to make sure, I will sleep with my sister."

"Have no fear, David is here. And I will sleep with both of them!"

Karen laughed. Kate began to giggle.

"Dad," Steve sounded serious. "You should know me better than that."

"Yes, you should, at three in the morning when we're all asleep, they'll go out in the garage and bang," Eddie said.

"Well, anyway, I've said what I had to say." Bruce began to chuckle as he went back to the driver's side.

"Yes, outstanding statement. Like the Gettysburg Address, right to the point," Eddie said. "Wouldn't you agree, Dave?"

"Absolutely. And, Dad, when you get to Napa, don't forget to sleep on the couch."

Bruce, laughing, put his head over his right shoulder and backed out of the driveway.

They were in bed and their arms were around each other. There was no need to talk. They were content to be close together.

"I'm glad about Karen and Steve," Bruce finally said.

"Yes, I am too," Kate said.

"It's kind of like you and me, in a way."

"I know," she said.

Many minutes passed. She cried quietly.

135

He hugged her tightly. "What's the matter?"
"You'll come back to me, darling. Won't you?"
"Yes, I'll come back," he said.

Chapter Fifteen

The Rolls Royce left the San Francisco International Airport and entered the Bay Shore Freeway going south during normal traffic hours. The driver sought the Peninsula Avenue turnoff in Burlingame. Their course would then be west across El Camino Real and into the Hillsborough section.

The driver was middle aged, five foot nine, slim, baldish hair that was beginning to turn gray. A scar was over his right eye that penetrated the eyebrow. His narrow lips rarely smiled. The man next to him was younger, twenty-nine, six foot three inches, 182 pounds, with a full head of black straight hair parted on the right. His facial features were perfectly chiseled with a narrow nose, slightly sunken cheeks, and full lips. He was considered handsome and he could have been nominated for the All Italian American Man, except he had a vicious nature, and he was very deadly with almost any small weapon, including his hands.

The lone passenger in the rear seat was Eduardo DeLucci, protege of Vincent Moroni, and a powerful influence in the Costa Nostra. DeLucci was sixty years old and he was fifty pounds overweight for his five foot six inch frame. His hair was completely gray with no evidence of balding, and his eyebrows were heavy and darker than his hair. His face was full, his cheeks being rounded and fat. His torso was short and his stomach protruded. Tailoring made his clothes fit to perfection and conceal a good deal of the excessive indulgence. A light gray suit and vest with light blue shirt and dark blue tie complemented his wavy gray hair. A two carat diamond on a platinum setting was on the ring finger of each hand. A simple gold wedding band was worn as a necklace.

The Rolls Royce entered the grounds and went to the wide steps by the front door. DeLucci leaned forward. "Gerald," he said to the younger man. "Come with me. If I go into a room with the old man, stay outside that room, but close. If anyone

Glenn Mathews

talks to you, do not incite anger. Show patience and calmness. If I need you, I will call you."

"Yes, sir."

DeLucci looked at the back of the driver's head. "I want you out of the car, too, Jim. Stay near the car, but be on the steps' side. Be relaxed, stay calm, act like I'm visiting an old friend. But be ready if we need you."

"Yes, sir."

All three men got out of the car.

The front door opened. "Eduardo," Moroni shouted from his wheelchair. "My son, how pleased I am to see you." The old man wore a dark blue pinstripe and a white shirt with red tie.

Charlie Dobbs stood behind him.

"Ah, padrone, you look so well," DeLucci said. "I get fatter, you get younger. I have missed you." He shook Moroni's hand, and held it with both hands for a moment.

Moroni chuckled. "You always were the truthful one." They entered the foyer.

"Charlie, leave us, Eduardo will wheel me into the living room."

DeLucci went behind the old man and began to push.

"The room over there to your right."

"I remember, and I would wager, padrone, that the bar is still in the living room, and the bourbon and soda is still your daily libation. Pardon me, bourbon with just a trace of soda."

"You never forget anything. Do you, Eduardo?"

"Not much, but I"m particularly adept at being a bartender." They entered the room and DeLucci closed the double doors.

Gerald sat on a wooden chair near the doors. Charlie Dobbs sat on the second step of the staircase. They watched one another.

"Are you the one they call Gerald?" Dobbs said.

"I am the one."

"You're supposed to be the best, at everything." Dobbs smirked.

"No, that is incorrect, I am just the second best," Gerald replied dutifully. "A Charlie Dobbs is the best, he works for Mister Moroni."

"I'm Charlie Dobbs."

"A great pleasure to know you, Charlie, if I may call you Charlie. I have heard a great deal about you." Gerald had a respectful expression.

Dobbs stood and glared at the younger man. He left the entry hall and headed for the kitchen.

DeLucci served the old man's highball, and poured himself a glass of red wine. He sat opposite Moroni.

"I haven't seen you for a longtime," DeLucci said. "You haven't been east for two years. The others keep asking about you. You don't even go into Vegas."

"The operations run smoothly without my presence. All over the country. If they didn't, I'd go where I'm needed. You should be aware of that by now."

"We are, padrone, we are. You needn't get angry."

"And I haven't seen you for awhile. You don't come to visit me like you did," the old man scolded.

"I have been very busy, padrone. Someone has to make the detailed decisions. You did once, but now you have assigned that job to me. I go everywhere --"

"How are your wife and daughters?" the old man interrupted.

"They are fine, padrone, and they send you their love. Sylvia, I believe, is a little heavier, but I am not one to criticize. Our daughters are healthy and quite lovely. Both are married now, and two months ago we became grandparents for the first time. Angela gave birth to a baby boy."

"You sit down and immediately you want to talk business. Your family should be important to you. You have one. I have nothing but a wanton ex-wife who is a terrible influence on Edward and Karen." Moroni squirmed in his chair. He drank half his highball.

"Her influence is so bad that they only have disrespect for me. So I have disinherited them. I no longer have a son or

139

Glenn Mathews

daughter. But you, you have a family. You have a wife and children. You should respect them and talk about them. But all you think about is the business. The organization. That is wrong."

"You are quite right, and I apologize. But I have suffered with you when I heard of your family problems. You are aware of that. And I have always been there for you, whenever you needed me."

"I need no one!"

"We all need someone, padrone," DeLucci said quietly. "I have needed you many times. You have needed me at times. My allegiance to you will never change."

"The only savior I have is God. He guides me!"

"I am glad, padrone. I have heard that you have become religious, and I am happy and pleased for you."

"Why did you come here?"

"To visit with you. As you said, our last meeting was a longtime ago. We needed to see each other."

"You want me to step down. Don't you? That's why you're here." Moroni bent down even lower and looked up at him suspiciously. "You're not here to see me as a friend. And you were my dearest friend. You were like a son to me." The old man whined. "Now, suddenly, you want me to give up my leadership. After all these years. You have turned against me. All of you have turned against me. You want to force me out."

"Force is not the proper word, padrone."

"What else is it? Why are you here?" The old man sounded angry.

"I came here to see you. To make sure that you are well, and to find out if I could do anything for you," DeLucci said calmly. "Secondly, I came here to make a reasonable request."

"Request?" The old man laughed softly. "You have a way with words, Eduardo. You can twist things to your own satisfaction."

"There is no need to twist things, or have a way with words when dealing with the truth."

140

"Truth? Truth about me? What truth?"

"You are elderly, padrone. Your leadership in the family will never be equaled. But it is time to rest. To forget about decisions. To reap the benefits of your wisdom by retiring now. You are a very wealthy man. Truly, enjoy your life now, and your God. Let me take over, padrone. You have taught me well. I know what to do. The leaders wish this. I want you to retire, too."

There was a long silence.

The old man stared at the folded hands in his lap. "And, if I don't retire?"

There was no response.

"I can make things very difficult. I do have loyal followers," the old man threatened.

"You are too intelligent, padrone, to allow that to happen. Nothing would be gained."

There was a lengthy pause. "Get me another drink, Eduardo," the old man said, submissiveness in the voice.

DeLucci returned with the drink, again sitting opposite Moroni.

"What else, Eduardo? Surely there is more to my resigning."

"Yes, there is. Upon resigning, you are to receive one hundred thousand dollars monthly, a cash retirement benefit, and all your household expenses, including employment, will be paid for."

"I accept," the old man said.

"You will resign?"

"Yes."

"When?" DeLucci said.

"Now."

"Your word, padrone, has always been your bond."

"Yes, always. Are you doubting my word now?" the old man said. He seemed angry.

"No, padrone." DeLucci reached inside his coat and retrieved a thick business envelope. He handed the envelope to Moroni. "The first of your retirement benefits."

The old man nodded. He stuck the envelope into a crevice in the chair, alongside his leg.

"There is one more request. With your permission, padrone, I must be frank."

The old man smiled. "Go ahead. You're asking, of course."

"Yes." DeLucci paused. "Your ex-wife, padrone, we ask that you leave her alone now, and all those associated with her."

"I will deal with my ex-wife as I see fit. Now, tomorrow, or whenever. Is that clear." Moroni was very angry.

"Then deal with her and be done with it." DeLucci raised his voice for the first time. "But leave others out of it. You involve us. This situation is too risky. We do not need investigations. Be done with it."

The old man made an about-face. He began to cry quietly. "I can't," he sobbed. "I love her too much. I can't harm her."

DeLucci waited a few moments. He leaned forward in the chair. "Does your ex-wife know anything about your leadership in the organization? Anything that could incriminate us?"

The old man stopped crying. He thought for a longtime. "I have the situation under control. If she began to incriminate me, she would no longer incriminate me. I could act then." He paused. "When I die, it may be necessary to--." He shrugged. "A reasonable length of time may be necessary. The deed should not be obvious."

"I understand," DeLucci said.

Chapter Sixteen

Moroni sat on a padded bench in the locker room of a therapeutic clinic in Palo Alto. He had been going every Tuesday to this same clinic for over two years. Therapists, baths, pool exercise, massages, or general treatment for his legs could be obtained closer to his home, but these other places did not have a Mickey, or a Claudia. Both were extremely competent and each knew what they were doing. Both knew how to prolong pleasure.

They were alone in the locker room and Mickey helped the old man to dress. She was a brunette and had a man's haircut, twenty-two, barely over five feet with slim arms and legs, and waistline. Her bosom was large. Her lips were full and could form a pout easily, or blow a kiss sensually.

"Get my wallet out of the locker," the old man snapped. He no longer had a hard-on and he wanted to go home.

"Here it is, honey." She handed him the wallet.

He took five one hundred dollar bills out of the wallet and gave them to her. The old man felt she was worth every penny. She could prolong his coming for a longtime, and when it did happen, she enjoyed the fluid spurting into her mouth. Can't say that about a lot of women, he thought. He much preferred a blow job rather than fucking. Fucking was too much strain on him now, and it really didn't give him as much pleasure.

"Thank you, sweetie, you're very generous. You always are," Mickey said. "I wish you had an erection now. I'd do it for nothing!"

The old man smiled. Do it for nothing, he thought. Sure. There isn't a cunt that would suck cock for nothing, or fuck. They always want something. He was convinced that any cunt anywhere in the world would suck his cock, if the price was right. Women are all wanton. Simple as that.

143

Glenn Mathews

"That's a nice thought," he said. "But we'll wait until next week. Next week, I want to spend more time in the pool. My legs need the exercise."

"Okay. Claudia will be here next week, too. Then later we'll have some fun with you. Okay?"

"That will be nice."

He was dressed, and Mickey helped him into the wheelchair. She wheeled him out of the locker room and into a hallway that led to a fire exit, a small door that opened to a pathway leading to the curb of a residential section. The building was one level, there were no steps, and Mickey had no problem maneuvering him through the door and to the pathway. The old man's driver met them on the concrete path.

"Goodbye, my child, until next week."

"Goodbye, Mister Moroni." Mickey blew him a kiss and went inside the building.

The driver was a big man, but not fat. He had a chunky body, like a wrestler, a large head almost bald, two inches under six feet, middle aged, and he was a killer. He wheeled the old man down the path and toward the black Fleetwood Cadillac by the curb. As they neared the sidewalk Moroni noticed a blind man walking towards them.

"Stop," the old man said. They had yet to reach the sidewalk. He wanted to inspect the blind man.

The blind man was an older person, about six feet tall, a little overweight, dark stubble, and wore a dirty Gatsby cap. He had on sunglasses and dirty white tennis shoes. His clothes were unkempt, dirty, and faded blue denim trousers, and a blue plaid shirt that was wrinkled and soiled. An old brown sweater hung loosely on his frame. In his left hand he carried a white cane with a red tip which he tapped occasionally on the sidewalk. In his right hand he held a leash that was attached to a scuffed leather halter that went around the shoulders and under the chest of an old black dog. The dog stayed right next to the leg with its head just beyond the knee.

"Go now," the old man ordered his bodyguard and driver.

144

The wheelchair moved in front of the blind man, three feet from a collision.

The black dog quickly moved in front of his master's leg.

The blind man stopped. He looked over Moroni's head and stared at the tie on the driver's shirt. "Is anybody there?"

"Yes. Yes, and I am sorry to be in your way," the old man replied. "What a wonderful dog you have. He stopped you from running into us."

"Yes, she is pretty good, all right," the blind man said. His voice sounded old with a cackling sound. "Like me, old Bessie here is getting old, but she still does her job." The black dog cocked her head.

"We all get old," the old man said. He took a hundred dollar bill from his wallet and handed it to the driver. "Give that to him."

The driver left the wheelchair and placed the bill into the blind man's right hand. "That's a hundred dollar bill, old-timer."

"Well, now, thank you, sir. Thank you," the blind man responded. "I guess there are two of you, and I thank you both."

The old man waved the driver to move and he pushed the wheelchair to the rear door of the Cadillac. The driver helped the old man onto the rear seat, shut the rear door, and deposited a folded wheelchair into the trunk of the vehicle. The driver opened the front door and got into the car. As he closed the door, the blind man rushed to the rear door and opened it.

Bruce was in the back and, leash dragging, Christy followed him.

She jumped over the back of the front seat and landed next to the driver, growling viciously, her teeth bared.

Bruce pushed Moroni to the end of the seat, the side of his head hit the window.

"You hurt me. Goddamn you!" Moroni yelled.

Bruce shut the door. He said to the driver quietly, "You close the window between us or reach for that gun I see, you're a dead man. I'll have her tear your throat out." He raised his voice. "Is that clear?"

"Yes, yes." The driver stared wide-eyed at the dog.

Bruce reached over the seat and pulled out a forty-five pistol from the driver's shoulder holster. "Put your hands behind your neck. Watch him, Christy."

The dog moved an inch closer to his neck, her growl even more threatening.

Bruce looked at Moroni. "Take your pants down. I'm going to stick this hundred dollar bill you gave me right up your ass."

"Fuck you," the old man hollered.

Bruce hit Moroni on the side of the head with the forty-five. The old man winced. He was in pain. The blow drew blood above the ear but was not delivered hard enough to do serious damage.

"Take your pants down, slime."

"I'm an old man," Moroni whined, "please do not hurt me anymore. I'll give you anything you want." He began slowly to unbuckle his belt.

"Take your time, slime, we got all-day. You have a bullet proof, soundproof car, and dark glass that nobody can see inside. You just take your time." Bruce glanced at the driver. Christy seemed in control.

Bruce took the top of Moroni's open pants and pulled hard, and continued to pull. Pants and underwear came over the knees. He held Moroni by the throat with his right hand and reached under the right cheek with his left hand holding the bill. He pushed the bill through the anus and into the rectum.

Moroni screamed.

Bruce kept pushing the bill. "How do you like the pain, Mister Moroni?" Bruce kept pushing, three of his fingers were inside Moroni's rectum.

Moroni continued to scream. He no longer controlled his bowels. Diarrhea splattered out. Moroni fainted.

Bruce removed his fingers. The bill remained partially embedded. He opened the built-in liquor cabinet and poured half a decanter of bourbon over his hands, wiping them on Moroni's pants. The odor in the car was sickening. He slapped Moroni hard on the cheeks, several times.

The old man opened his eyes. He breathed heavily.

Bruce glanced at the driver. Christy lowered her growl, but the intent in her eyes remained vicious. She had him scared.

"You should feel at home," Bruce said to Moroni. "You're nothing but a stinking piece of shit, and you've made life miserable for a lot of people."

The old man was horrified, and in complete disarray.

"Now listen to me, slime, and listen good," Bruce demanded. "I want to see your henchman. The bum you call Charlie Dobbs. The bum you sent to kill Homer and his family. You remember Homer. Don't you? You knew him as Smitty. You like to kill children. Don't you, Moroni? Makes you feel like a big important man." Bruce slapped him again. "Then you sent this bum to beat up and later kill a pharmacist. The --"

Moroni shook his head.

"What did you say, Moroni?" Bruce slammed his head against the window.

"Please, please," the old man whined, and he began to nod his head.

"You sent this same bum to kill Stanley Stevens, your ex father-in-law. This is for Stanley." Bruce slapped him hard. "You also sent another bum, a Filipino, to kill me, but he didn't quite make it."

The old man stared at him in disbelief. Then the horror came. "What is your name," he whispered.

"Bruce Campbell. Mean anything to you, Moroni?"

The old man glared at him. Anger was his only emotion now.

"Are you listening good, slime?" Bruce said. "Send me Charlie Dobbs. I'll be in Oregon, you know where. We have a score to settle. Do you understand me?"

"Yes," he said hoarsely.

"And then I'll be back for you, Moroni. I'm going to kill you," Bruce said. "You're going to have to wait for me, but I'll be back. I want you to enjoy your wait. Did you hear me, slime?" he yelled.

The old man nodded.

"I said did you hear me, slime?" Bruce yelled.

"Yes," he said hoarsely.

Bruce looked at the driver who sat sideways on the front seat. Christy's black nose was an inch from his throat.

"When we get out of this car, you leave in a hurry. Don't dawdle, or you're dead!"

"I'll leave, I'll leave!" the driver shouted.

He faced the old man. Moroni's eyes were half closed and they glared at him in hate. "Enjoy your stink," Bruce said. "You belong together." He opened the backdoor and stepped out. "Come on, Christy." The Lab jumped over the back of the seat and joined her master outside the car. Bruce slammed the door.

The motor started and the Cadillac left quickly. Moroni tried to yell and scream but he did not have the strength. He was in shock but he didn't know that. He pounded his fists on the shoulders of the driver. "You son of a bitch," his voice was low and hoarse. "You fucking son of a bitch, you didn't help me. Get me to Charlie. Get me to Charlie. I'm going to kill that bastard. He's dead. He's dead!"

Bruce and Christy walked back to George. The Suburban was parked around the corner, a block from the clinic. They got on the front seat and Bruce removed the halter and leash from the dog. He retrieved a towel from the floor and wiped off most of the charcoal over his stubble. He gave Christy a hug. "Well now, Bessie, we didn't do too bad back there." Christy looked at him. Bruce laughed, and gave her another hug. "Glad you didn't correct me, we had to fool them. Besides we won't use that name again. I like Christy better."

He started the truck and they left. "We'll get back to Napa and get the trailer ready and we'll leave for Oregon in the morning," Bruce said. Christy sat on the passenger side and looked out the windshield. She panted. "We may have taken on more than we can chew, Christy, but we'll have the home field advantage. He's coming to us, and we'll be ready."

What Bruce did not know was that Dobbs had left that night for Oregon.

Chapter Seventeen

At seven in the morning an older Chevrolet sedan was parked near a trailer long enough to unload necessary supplies. Ten minutes were allowed to break into the trailer and deposit a duffel bag and two brown grocery bags. Dobbs used care opening the aluminum door on the trailer . A crowbar was all that was necessary but he did not want dents and scratches to appear obvious, particularly to Campbell when he arrived. The vehicle was then driven a half mile to a small and rarely used picnic area by the South Umpqua River, and parked behind a group of heavy bushes. Charlie Dobbs returned to the trailer on foot.

Dobbs knew what to expect when he arrived at Campbell's home by the river. Smitty, and others hired to watch her lover, had told him about the trailer pad and the trailer at the other end of the property. An isolated neighbor informed one of his men that the trailer was rarely used except for a few weeks in the late summer. Should the owners show up earlier than usual, there would be no problem killing them. Arrival of the victim was anticipated for late afternoon or early evening. He knew Campbell would not be later. Consequently, during the wait, comfort was of primary concern.

Dobbs took his time inspecting the interior of the twenty-five foot trailer, and there was much to like. A bathroom was at the rear, twin beds in the middle of the rig, and a kitchen and large dinette in the front. As anticipated, the trailer had been completely winterized, all water, electric, and propane had been shut off.

Dobbs began to get organized. He had the trailer functional within forty minutes. He didn't bother with the utilities, having brought a kerosene lamp, two and a half gallons of water, and twenty-five pounds of ice for the refrigerator. He emptied the grocery bags but left the duffel bag intact. All his equipment was in there.

The old man had been very insistent and specific that the limbs and cock were to be cut off from the torso, and all five pieces were to be buried separately on the Tiller property. The old fart wanted the head, and Dobbs had a hunch it would be going to the ex.

The dog was to be gutted and left in the woods for the vultures. "Why the big deal over a fucking dog?" he wondered aloud.

Bruce and Christy arrived at 5:15 p.m. with almost two and one half hours of daylight remaining. Enough time, Bruce figured, to get the rig detached from George and permanently placed on the pad. He began to back the trailer, but stopped. He looked around the property. He believed all was peaceful as a churchyard, and he smiled when he saw the familiar river and creek.

The venetian blinds were closed but Charlie Dobbs opened one slat at eye level so he could watch the proceedings with binoculars.

For three hours Bruce Campbell was busy getting his trailer set up. After detaching and connecting utilities and septic, he took long cable type wiring from the satellite dish in the yard and pushed the end of the coated wire through an opening over a wheel and under the living room. He went to the shed and returned carrying two electronic devices to the living room. He was in the trailer for almost an hour getting the television operational.

Christy went outside, making her rounds. She was near the owner's trailer. She went to the front of the smaller trailer and sniffed around the propane tanks. She went around the trailer twice. She growled softly, and then went to the parking section by the road.

"Christy, come on in here. Time for dinner," Bruce yelled.

The dog returned and entered the rear door of her trailer. "Keep alert now," Bruce said. "You're going to let me know when he arrives."

151

Lights came on inside, and the front shade was raised so a viewer could look into the kitchen. Dobbs saw him making sandwiches, and he noted that he was a tea drinker.

"Not a bad looking trailer," Dobbs muttered, "but I'd get myself a bigger one and a better one, and a newer truck to pull it." He thought traveling and living in an RV was a good way to retire. He glanced at his watch and noted that ten was over an hour away. He decided to eat some coffee cake and have a glass of milk.

Charlie Dobbs was told that the black dog went outside every night around ten before retiring. At nine-forty he left the trailer. He carried a baseball bat and a forty-five was tucked halfway under his belt. The night-light was on and illuminated most of the yard. Walking slowly and quietly, he stayed within the shadows. He arrived at the pump house near the steps leading to the parking pad. Twenty minutes went by before the rear door opened, and the black dog exited.

"Goddamn," Dobbs swore to himself, "the dog is going down the steps to the yard on the other side of the trailer. Wait a minute, the bitch could come around the rear shed and into this yard when she's through taking a shit." He moved further back and peeked out from a corner of the pump house. He saw her momentarily. He moved his head back, and waited a moment. He scratched the ground softly with the end of the baseball bat, and then raised the bat in the air. He waited. He was about to lower the bat to relax the muscles when he heard the growl, close by, inches from him, just around the corner. Dobbs' arms were tired and shook a bit from holding the bat high above him, but he was determined. He saw the head, and the eyes barely turned to him when the blow struck her over the right ear.

Christy lay unconscious. The blow came so fast that she had no opportunity to bark, or even whimper.

Dobbs crawled from the pump house and along the bottom of the foundation near the side where the two trailer doors were located. At the end of the raised foundation, by the rear shed, he stood and quietly walked around the shed, into the other yard, and up the steps by the front of the trailer. Still holding the baseball bat, he went quickly along the other side of the trailer to the back area near the spare tire rack. The night-light barely reached that location and the area was much darker. He waited. He knew Campbell would be calling for his dog.

Bruce opened the rear exit. "Come on, Christy, time to come in," he hollered through the screen door. "Come on, girl." He waited. "Christy?" He turned off the light in the bedroom, left the entry for a moment, turned off all the lights in the trailer, and returned holding a forty-five in his right hand, the same pistol taken from Moroni's driver. Slowly, he opened the screen door and went down the two metal steps. He started for the stairs near the pump house when the blow landed.

Bruce felt the terrible pain for an instant, and then he blacked out. His body fell on the concrete beyond the artificial grass. His right arm dangled over the edge of the trailer pad, the gun fell from his hand into a large fern on the ground at the bottom of the foundation.

"Never had an easier job," Dobbs mumbled to himself. "Shit, why he causes so much trouble is beyond me. Getting old, too. No sweat."

He dragged the body by the heels, down the concrete steps by the pump house, and onto the grass where the night-light was effective. He examined the body near a small tree. "Colder than a mackerel," he mumbled. "I'll wait until morning to kill him and cut him up. He'll be easier to work on if he's fresh and, besides, I'm too tired now."

He went to the owner's trailer and returned with the duffel bag. He tied Campbell's wrists tightly behind his back, brought rope from the wrists that went around the trunk of the small tree to the ankles and tied the ankles together, the torso being on the other side of the tree. He liked his work. "If he can get out of that, he's a magician!"

Dobbs was anxious to see the inside of Campbell's trailer, but first he wanted to examine the dog. He returned to the rear of the pump house. "Out cold. Not much breath. She won't last long. I'll gut her in the morning, too." The duffel bag was left by the dog.

He walked to the rear door of the trailer and reached inside to the wall, found the light switch and turned on a bedroom light. Dobbs went to the light pole by the pump house, opened the switch box and turned off the night-light. He returned to the trailer.

The refrigerator and freezer were a sight to behold. Frozen chocolate bars, ice cream, chocolate syrup, cake, and fruit. Much better, Dobbs thought, than plain old coffee cake. And, there were bacon and eggs. He'd have a nice breakfast in the morning before all that work. He turned on the television and scanned the stations.

"My God, he's got Showtime," he exclaimed out loud. "Way out here." Dobbs was delighted, a horror movie was about to begin in three minutes. He'd just get some dessert and make himself comfortable on the couch, watch a movie, and later get a little shut-eye. "The bastard sure knew how to live." Dobbs laughed. "Up until now, that is!"

The weather was chilly at four in the morning on a late spring day. The cold and the brisk breeze that was present can help revive a person, even an animal.

Christy opened her eyes. Blood had coagulated over and down her ear, and there was still a slight glistening from fresh blood. A lump had formed, about half the size of an egg, on the skull just above the ear. Still laying down, she shook her head, again, and again. She stood, her legs were wobbly. Her movement was slow and clumsy but she did not have far to go. She found him.

Bruce lay on his left side, the small of his back against the tree trunk, his legs and arms around the sides of the trunk with one foot of taut rope between the ankles and wrists. He was still unconscious.

Christy lay next to his right cheek and began to lick that portion of his face. She licked for nearly twenty minutes. His eyes began to flutter. She whimpered.

Bruce was dazed. He blinked his eyes several times. He had a bad headache. He remembered what happened to him, and he became aware of his predicament. A smile came, his dog had her head on his neck, and her tail wagged slightly.

"Christy, listen to me," Bruce whispered slowly.

The dog raised her head, moved back a few inches, and looked at her master.

"Go to the shed and get me the clippers, the yard clippers in the shed." He was almost certain the shed door was still open, he had not returned to close it when he got the satellite receiver and de-scrambler.

Christy was unsteady but she slowly got to the shed. The door was open and the interior was dark, but she knew where the clippers were kept, on a nail near the door. She found them with her nose. She took one of the rubber handles in her mouth and, with difficulty, pulled the clippers off the nail. She carried them to her master and laid them by his stomach.

"Put the clippers in my hands," Bruce whispered very slowly, and he moved his head toward the tree. He had been exercising his fingers and hands and the numbness was nearly gone.

Christy brought the clippers to his hands and Bruce was able to grab the rubber handles with his right hand. He squeezed the handles quickly and repeatedly forcing the clasp to loosen and separate. The blades sprang open. The clippers were nine inches long with four inch blades.

"Now what?" Bruce mumbled to himself and Christy. "There's no give in that damn rope to my ankles. I can't bring my hands and feet closer together, and I can't get the blades to cut it."

"Christy, go and hold the clippers," Bruce whispered.

The dog cocked her head.

"Take the clippers," he said.

Christy went behind him and took the clippers out of his hand and brought them to his stomach, but she did not drop them.

"Yes, hold the clippers," Bruce nodded, "but back there." He moved his head toward the tree.

The dog returned to his hands and Bruce was able to place the rope from the wrists to the ankles between the blades. He began to move the rope backward and forward over the cutting edge. He had very little give to work with but there was movement on the blade.

Christy dropped the clippers.

"That's okay, girl. Pick up the clippers and hold the clippers," he whispered.

Christy picked them up three times, but dropped them when Bruce began to move the rope over the blade. She finally grasped one of the handles tightly in her mouth and placed the blades so that the rope was between them.

Bruce, with a little body English, a little movement on the blade, and with continued and patient effort, got the rope severed in thirty minutes. Using the tree and his hands and back for support, he raised himself to his knees.

"Good girl. Keep holding the clippers, Christy," he said slowly and softly. He snapped his fingers and looked over his shoulder. "Bring the clippers to my hands." He waited. "Good girl. Hold the clippers."

He worked on one section of rope over his wrists. The movement on the blade was greater than before and Christy held the clippers firmly. In twenty minutes, the hands and wrists were free. He sat against the tree trunk. Christy dropped the clippers and put her head on his lap. He patted and hugged her.

Across the river the first inkling of dawn peeked over the mountain. Bruce had the clippers and surprise for his weapons. He saw the duffel bag by the pump house. He was about to examine its contents when something shiny caught his eye. The fern by the foundation had an object in it. The fern had been partially trampled by Dobbs when he crawled away from the pump house.

"Could it be?" he mumbled excitedly.

Bruce crawled to the fern and retrieved the forty-five pistol.

He decided to keep the rope tied around his ankles. He placed the clippers, and the rope that had been removed, under the fern. He went back to the tree and placed his legs around the side of the trunk, and his loose hands held the forty-five behind his back and around the other side of the trunk. His head lay on the ground, on the left cheek. He was in position.

"Christy, go back behind the shed and stay out of sight."

The Lab cocked her head.

"Go on, girl, stay out of sight. Don't come until I call you. Go behind the shed," Bruce said quietly.

With a sorrowful look, Christy left. She went to the river, not the shed.

Fifteen minutes later, Bruce heard movement inside the trailer. In a little while, he smelled bacon.

Charlie Dobbs left the trailer a half hour later, and went down the stairs by the pump house. He looked at Campbell. "So, you're awake, eh?"

"Yeah. You're Dobbs?" Bruce recognized him from photographs Billy had shown him.

"That's me."

"You got here ahead of me. Didn't you?"

"Yeah."

"Like your reputation says, pretty smart," Bruce said.

"I get well paid to be smart. If I couldn't outsmart you, I wouldn't be worth a shit," Dobbs said. He went around the pump house. "Where's your fucking dog?"

"I don't know. You tell me. What did you do to her, Dobbs?"

"I knocked her skull in two. She should be laying here dead."

"I hope not," Bruce said.

"No matter, I'll find her. I'll work on you now." Dobbs began to remove articles from the duffel bag.

"Can I ask you some questions?" Bruce said.

"Make them short."

"You killed that pharmacist. Didn't you?"

"I'll save us some time, asshole. I killed all the people you talked to Mister Moroni about, including those fucking brats, and their mother. And I enjoyed myself." Dobbs walked to him and dumped saws and knives by him. He returned to the duffel bag.

"You're a rotten human being," Bruce said.

"I'll just kill you a little slower for that," Dobbs said. He removed the extension cord and started for the trailer to attach the end to an outside plug.

"Mind if I tell you a little story about yourself?"

"Go ahead, asshole, you got a minute or two left. I like a good story," Dobbs said.

"Have you heard of Aesop's fable about the hare and the tortoise?" Bruce said.

"Speak English," Dobbs said.

"Aesop was a storyteller from long ago, and every tale had a moral to it," Bruce said. "A hare is a rabbit, and a tortoise is a turtle. The turtle challenged the smart aleck rabbit to a race knowing he could beat him. The rabbit laughed in his face and told the --"

"I know the story, asshole, I saw a cartoon about it. Damn dumb, a turtle would never beat a rabbit." Dobbs was at the duffel bag again and removed a portable electric saw.

"That's where you're wrong. You're like the rabbit, Dobbs."

"What do you mean, asshole?"

"You took your time about killing us. You enjoyed prolonging it, just like the rabbit. You enjoyed the wait, Dobbs, entertaining yourself. You underestimated your opponents. You really are a stupid bastard, Dobbs. Christy!"

Bruce moved both arms from behind the tree. The right hand held the pistol. He grasped the gun with both hands, and aimed.

Christy appeared at the top of the pathway leading to the river. She advanced toward Dobbs, growling.

At first, Dobbs was shocked. He had the electric saw in his hand, but dropped it. He walked slowly toward Bruce. "You rotten motherfucker, I'll kill you with my bare hands!"

"The underdog won, Dobbs. So long, asshole!" Bruce aimed for the stomach and pulled the trigger.

Dobbs fell backwards. The bullet exited at the lower back leaving a large hole. He groveled on the ground, and staggered slowly to his feet.

"You son...of a..bitch, I'm ...going to kill ...you!" He advanced on Bruce.

Christy barked.

Dobbs reached for the pistol in his belt. Another bullet hit him in the chest, exited and left a large hole between the shoulder blades. Dobbs fell on his head and stomach.

Very slowly, he raised himself. On hands and knees he crawled toward Bruce.

"You...can't...kill me."

A third bullet hit him between the eyes, blowing out the back of his head. Dobbs' face hit the ground, his body fell over Bruce's knees.

Christy was inches from the dead face, and she kept barking at it. She continued to bark.

Bruce sat there, against the tree, his ankles still tied together, the body over his knees. "You can stop barking, Christy," he said quietly. "We don't have to worry about him anymore. But, man, what a mean bastard. He took a lot of killing."

Bruce began to tremble.

He wanted to be in Hillsborough by five that afternoon, and there were several things that needed doing before leaving the river site. As he worked, he began to think about the car that brought the killer.

Dobbs' body was placed on a large tarpaulin, covered, and dragged to the Suburban. The effort took all of Bruce's strength, but he got the body into the back of the vehicle. He kept a set of keys that he found in Dobbs' pocket.

He washed Christy's head, and cleansed the area with hydrogen peroxide. He would have a vet look at her in Sonoma.

He washed thoroughly, used peroxide on the back of his head, changed clothes, and swallowed four Motrin.

Bruce was suspicious, and he inspected Tom and Lois's trailer discovering that was where Dobbs hid before attacking them. He hurriedly cleaned their trailer and deposited all the food into a bag to haul to the refuse center nearby. He looked at the front door and was able to repair it, making sure the door locked firmly.

The knives, saws, and extension cord from the yard were put back into the duffel bag and into the shed. He straightened his trailer, packed a few articles, made them a lunch to take, and locked the trailer and shed.

They had driven a short way when Bruce turned left into a small picnic area.

"The only logical place to park a car if Dobbs didn't want anyone to know he was here," he said to Christy.

He drove slowly throughout the area and began to feel he was wrong. Then he saw chrome behind bushes.

Bruce got out of the car. He heard Christy whimper.

"Go ahead, you can take a swim."

Christy was in the water in four seconds.

He found a car, and the key from Dobbs' pocket fit the lock. He used another key for the trunk. Bruce inspected both interiors and couldn't find anything suspicious. He would call Billy and the vehicle would be impounded and given a thorough search. The trunk was locked and he was about to lock the car when he saw two remote control door openers on the visor. He took them, thinking they just might come in handy.

Fisher told him that a cook and housekeeper usually left the premises in separate cars around five in the afternoon. The Suburban was parked a half block from the expansive wrought iron gate to Moroni's estate. Bruce lowered the tailgate window, got out of the vehicle and lowered the tailgate. He took the leg end of the tarpaulin and pulled it toward him until a good portion of the contents overlapped the end of the tailgate. The overlap was like a board since rigor mortis had taken place. He uncovered the body, took an eight by eleven inch sheet of paper from his pocket and pinned it on the front of the corpse's shirt. He quickly covered the body and he walked to a large square brick column that supported one side of the gate, and waited. A small boulder was in his hand. He felt confident that one of the remote control units would open the gate, but that mitt wasn't going to be tipped. Not yet.

Two cars approached, and the gates automatically opened. When the gates were wide open he placed the boulder on the ground by the brick column hoping the inner rail of the gate would run into it and stop the gate from closing.

Bruce ran back to George and got behind the wheel. He started the truck and waited. When both cars had exited he drove through the opening of the gate just as they were beginning to close. George went up the drive and around the outer circle and stopped by the front door steps, motor running.

Bruce climbed to the rear of the vehicle, took the head end of the tarpaulin and raised it high. The corpse fell stiffly to the driveway. Bruce got behind the wheel, and with horn blaring and Christy barking, they headed for the outer gate. The opening between the gates was more than they needed.

"That boulder worked like a charm, Christy. Worked like a charm," Bruce yelled excitedly.

Two barks were the only reply.

Moroni's hands shook as he talked to DeLucci on the phone.
"What is it, padrone? What is the problem?" DeLucci said.
"He's going to kill me," the old man whined into his phone.
"Who is going to kill you?"
"Her lover. That woman most foul. Her lover."
"Why is he going to kill you?" DeLucci said.

Glenn Mathews

"Because he said so. And he killed Charlie. My Charlie. He killed him," the old man sobbed.

"What did he say to you?" DeLucci said calmly.

"He dumped Charlie's body by my doorstep with a note pinned to him, and I have the paper right here."

"What does it say?" DeLucci said patiently.

"'You're next, Moroni!'" the old man read. "'I'll be coming!'"

"Why did this man have Charlie's body?"

There was a long pause on the phone. The old man became angry. "Why all these questions? No one questions me."

"You need help, padrone. Don't you?"

A pause. "Yes," he said meekly.

"Why did this man have Charlie's body?" DeLucci repeated.

"I sent Charlie to take care of him," the old man said quietly. His voice became angry again. "Her lover attacked me in my car outside the clinic where I go for my legs. He slapped me hard many times, and threatened me. He had a vicious dog with him, too. I sent Charlie to kill them."

There was no response for several moments. "I'll send Gerald to protect you," DeLucci said. "He'll take a flight out tomorrow."

"Gerald? Who is this Gerald?"

"The younger man who was with me when I visited you," DeLucci said.

"That punk? He's nothing but a young punk!"

"Hardly. That punk, as you call him, is the best there is," DeLucci said quietly. "He'll stay with you until the deed is done."

"What happens if he comes tonight, or tomorrow morning? Before Gerald gets here!"

"He won't, he'll want to worry you awhile. Goodbye, padrone."

"Goodbye, Eduardo, my son." There was relief in the old man's voice.

DeLucci replaced the phone receiver. He looked across his desk at Gerald. "I have a job for you."

Chapter Eighteen

Gerald Puccinelli Grandinetti was his full name. Gerald was the only name permitted. Anyone calling him anything else, including profane names, was corrected only once.

Gerald arrived at the Moroni estate at one in the afternoon. He wore an off-white linen suit with a blue dress shirt, red tie, and black shoes. The housekeeper showed him into the living room, and left, closing the doors. The old man was seated in his wheelchair near the liquor cabinet. He had just made himself a drink. "You can sit down."

"No thank you, sir. I prefer to stand."

"You're Gerald?"

"Yes, sir."

"What's your last name?" Moroni said.

"Gerald is the only name I go by."

"Can you kill this guy?"

"You will have nothing to worry about, Mister Moroni," Gerald said. "I need to ask you some questions, however."

"All right. Go ahead."

"I will be with you until the matter is resolved. I need to know your habits. When you leave your home, for example."

"I go to my broker and bank on Mondays. My health clinic on Tuesday," the old man said.

"Then you won't be leaving here until this coming Monday?" Moroni nodded.

"Do you do anything here, at home, that is normally on schedule?"

"I take a nap, about two to four every afternoon. And I don't want to be disturbed."

"I need to be near you at all times, sir," Gerald said.

"You can take a room down the hall."

"Who else lives here, or works here? I must know everyone in your household," Gerald said.

"Why?"

"I would kill anyone else," Gerald said blandly.

"That's a good point." The old man was becoming impressed.

"I have a housekeeper, you saw her, a cook, a driver who also acts as a bodyguard, a valet, and he's a bodyguard, too. And a maid. Eh, she doesn't do much cleaning. Looks pretty, though."

"Who cleans this big house?" Gerald said.

"The housekeeper tidies up, but a cleaning outfit comes in every Wednesday, just the morning hours. And gardeners come, too. On Tuesday and Fridays, morning hours again, seven to twelve. They just left a little while ago," the old man said.

Does any other business come with regularity? Grocery, or floral deliveries, clothes cleaner, whatever," Gerald said.

"Not that I know of. The housekeeper and cook take care of those details."

"What about professional people? A lawyer, or a doctor, for example."

"No."

"Are you expecting anyone to visit you soon?" Gerald said.

"No."

"Who stays here overnight?"

"The driver and the valet. They each have a room over the garage," Moroni replied.

"When do the others leave?"

He was becoming impatient. "The cook and the housekeeper leave around five. The maid will sometimes stay overnight. She comes and goes as she pleases." The old man finished his drink. "Sit down, you're making me nervous."

Gerald smiled. He sat on a chair near Moroni. "Do you have a picture of this man?"

Moroni went to a desk, opened a drawer, wheeled to the chair and handed him a photograph.

Gerald studied the picture briefly. "Would you please call all your help now, so they can meet me and not question my presence."

"A good idea." Moroni wheeled to a wall and pressed a buzzer.

The pretty maid arrived. She continued to wear the short black dress with the white collar and the black hose. "Yes, Mister Moroni?"

"Get everyone here," Moroni ordered.

She glanced at the tall dark handsome man in the room. "Yes, sir."

After they arrived, the five of them stood respectfully in line, just inside the double doors.

"We're all here, Mister Moroni," the maid said. She smiled at Gerald.

"This man's name is Gerald," the old man addressed them. "He will be with us awhile. He is to come and go as he pleases. He is here to protect me. That's all you need to know." He thought a moment. "Unless Gerald has anything to say to you."

The driver and the valet had scowls. The valet was another Filipino, but a little older and much heavier than Roy.

They all watched Gerald.

"In order to familiarize myself with this property, I will be going everywhere," Gerald said. "With Mister Moroni's permission, I ask that no one leaves or enters this property without my knowledge, and that includes yourselves. That gate out there is not to be opened unless I know about it."

They all looked at Moroni.

The old man nodded. "That's right." He looked at the housekeeper. "You stay. All the rest of you can go now."

"Are you through?" Moroni asked Gerald when they had left.

"For now."

"Show this man to the room next to mine," Moroni said to the housekeeper.

She went to the double door exit. She smiled. "This way, sir." She was a short woman, plump, with a pleasing personality.

Gerald carried a large suitcase and followed her up the staircase. "Are you expecting any deliveries today, such as floral, grocery, or cleaners?"

"No, sir, not today," she said.

They entered a huge bedroom with a king-size bed. The furnishings were feminine.

"This was Mrs. Moroni's room until the divorce," she said.

Gerald placed the suitcase on the bed and opened it. The suitcase was empty except for a pair of black gloves, a pistol, a silencer, and a paper bag. Gerald put on the gloves, they fit tightly, and he screwed the silencer on the gun.

The housekeeper busied herself taking towels out of a bathroom cabinet and putting them on racks. She opened two pair of drapes and the sunlight rushed into the room. She turned and went towards Gerald. She stood on the other side of the bed and saw his hand come out of the suitcase. He held a gun. A second later, she was dead.

Gerald placed the gun in a holster behind his left lapel. He went casually down the stairs, saw the dining room to his right, crossed the room, pushed open the swinging door, and walked into an impressive kitchen.

The cook was getting a roast out of the refrigerator.

Gerald made a point to stand several feet from him. "If someone wanted to walk outside," Gerald said. "Where would he find the mechanism to open the gate?"

The cook laid a leg of lamb on the butcher block. "To walk out," he said, "there's a button under a plastic cover on the brick column to the right of the gate. Do you want to know where it is when you drive out?"

"That won't be necessary." Gerald removed the gun and shot the cook between the eyes.

He assumed a door in the laundry room would lead to a garage. Gerald opened the door and was surprised with the enormity of the garage. Four vehicles were inside, one space was vacant. The driver was polishing the hood of a black Cadillac.

"I need to talk to the valet. Can you tell me where he is?" Gerald said.

"I saw him go upstairs to his room," the driver said. "Go to the door at the other end, then use the outside stairs. Take the walkway to the second door on your left."

"Thank you."

The driver continued to wipe the car. "I don't know why that old man sent for you. He's got two professionals. We could have taken care of him."

As the driver worked and talked, Gerald walked behind the Cadillac, aimed, and shot the driver over the right ear just as the word 'him' was spoken.

Gerald went up the stairs and down the walkway to the second door. He knocked lightly, and the door was opened.

"I need to talk to you for a few moments. May I come in?"

The valet nodded with a grunt, and motioned him to a chair. Once seated, the valet stood directly in front of Gerald.

"Please, I wonder if you would step back a few feet. I have a phobia about people being too close to me," Gerald said.

The Filipino looked at him with disgust. He went to a chair several feet from the visitor. He saw the gun when he looked at him the next time.

Two bullets entered his chest.

"Besides, I don't want blood on this suit," Gerald said. He ejected the clip from the handgun, put it in his side coat pocket, and placed a full clip into the handle. He made sure the Filipino was dead.

Gerald returned to the garage and checked on the driver. He examined the cook in the kitchen. Both were dead. He went upstairs and examined the housekeeper.

Noises came from the room next to him.

He walked out the bedroom and went to his right in the hallway for several feet, to a door. Loud excited noises came from the room. He opened the door and saw the naked maid on top of a nude Moroni.

"We got it hard, honey. We got it hard," the maid said loudly.

Gerald shot the maid twice in the back.

167

She fell off Moroni to her right, on the bed.

His erection collapsed immediately.

"Goddamn, what is this?" Moroni saw Gerald take a few steps toward him, holding a gun. "Oh, my God. God save me. Please, dear God, save me!" the old man screamed.

"You have become bothersome, and a liability," Gerald said quietly. He shot the old man three times in the forehead.

Gerald always made sure his victims were dead. He left the bedroom, went next door, placed the gun, silencer, two clips, and the pair of gloves into the paper bag that was left in the suitcase. He closed the suitcase, grabbed it by the handle and went downstairs, and out the front door.

The day was clear and balmy and Gerald enjoyed the walk to the brick column. He pressed the button, and the gates opened. He walked down the road and he heard the gates shut behind him. He walked a mile to the main thoroughfare of El Camino Real and found a trash can. He put the paper bag from the suitcase into the container. He hailed a taxi and gave instructions to the airport. Once seated, he glanced at his wristwatch, the time was three o'clock. When he got home to New York he thought there would still be time to see John. He missed him terribly. He felt like he was falling in love.

Chapter Nineteen

They were doing the after dinner dishes. Kate rinsed and placed dishes and silverware in the dishwasher. Bruce cleaned off the table, wiped the range, and scrubbed a frying pan. They were not talking but each enjoyed the nearness to one another. Sally kept dropping a soft rubber toy nearby. The dogs were not permitted in the middle of the kitchen. When Bruce came near Sally he kicked the toy into the family room and she happily retrieved the little rubber dog, dropping it again and hoping for immediate attention. Christy was under and around the dinette table looking for crumbs or tiny scraps of food that may have fallen. She always found something, especially in the area where her master sat.

The doorbell rang and Kate opened the front door. William Fisher stood near the threshold. "Ms. Stevens, I"m Bill Fisher. We met here one evening a couple of years ago when I talked to you about your ex-husband."

"I remember. Come in, come in, Bill. May I call you Bill?"

"Please do, Kate?"

"Yes, I'd like that." She ushered him into the family room, past Bruce at the kitchen sink.

"Hi, Bruce," Fisher said as he walked through a portion of the kitchen.

"Good to see you, Billy. I'll be there in a minute," Bruce said.

"You take the big overstuffed leather chair and tell me how you like it, Bill," Kate said.

Fisher sat. "Outstanding. I'm here for the night."

They laughed. "You and I better be on a first name basis," Kate said. "I know you and Bruce are very close" She paused a moment. "I saw you at Dad's funeral. A long way off. You should have been with the group. Thank you for coming."

"I didn't know your dad, only through Bruce, but I wanted to pay my respects, and to see Bruce."

"There's some coffee left," Kate said.

"I'd like that." Christy lay beside Fisher and he patted the dog.

Kate returned with the coffee, Bruce followed. They sat on one of the sofas near Fisher. Sally lay on the floor between them. They watched him take a swallow and set the mug on the coffee table. He had a serious expression.

"What is it, Billy?" Bruce said.

"Moroni is dead." He paused a moment. "He was murdered yesterday afternoon."

Kate lay her head on the back of the sofa. "A terrible thing to say about someone's death but, thank God. He caused so much horror and pain." She took Bruce's hand and squeezed it hard.

"I'm very, very relieved," Bruce said quietly.

"You should be, you've had enough bumps and bruises!" Fisher scolded. "You and Christy are damn lucky to be alive. Baseball bats. Boots. Karate. Knives. Saws. Guns. For Christ's Sake, you didn't need to go after Moroni."

"How do you know I didn't?" Bruce said sheepishly.

"Because you wouldn't have killed three innocent people. In addition, two bodyguards are dead," Fisher said.

"What?" Kate gasped.

"That's right, six dead in all. You're going to read or hear about all this. The media is getting the details now. I thought it was better to come here and tell you myself," Fisher said. "A housekeeper, cook, and a maid were killed. We believe the maid was a prostitute permanently employed. And Moroni's driver and valet were killed. Those two also acted as bodyguards."

"Is this evil ever going to end?" Kate said sadly. "Why? Why?" She was becoming angry, and tears were beginning.

"I have no proof, but I know why," Fisher said. "Kate, what I'm about to say can't go any further. This discussion is just between the three of us."

"Why would I want to repeat anything so awful. It's all so shameful." Kate started to leave her seat. "However, if you want me out of the room, I'll go."

"Kate, that's not necessary," Fisher said.

She sat back.

"I had to request that or I could be severely reprimanded, and possibly out of a job if our talk went any further," Fisher said. "Please, Kate, I want you to stay. And there's something else I want you to know about."

She reached over and touched his hand. "I'm sorry."

Fisher smiled at her. "All six murders were committed by a professional. The organization, or the particular family, or the Mafia, if you will, wanted your ex-husband out of the way. His personal vendetta, you and those close to you, were causing an embarrassment and could bring trouble. No one wants an investigation, especially them. Also, Moroni's mental instability and senility upset them. So, the organization through their new leader, DeLucci, had him killed. The household, or those on the property at the time, had to be killed." He finished the coffee and placed the mug on the table.

"Quite simply, there could be no witnesses to Moroni's murder. Our New York office informed me that DeLucci has a personal bodyguard and hit man that made Charlie Dobbs look like a pantywaist. Of course, that I doubt. His name is Gerald, and that's the only name he goes by. New York suspects him of other murders. There's no question that the Moroni job fits his modus operandi. There's suspicion, too, that anytime DeLucci wants a personal hit made, without others knowing, he sends Gerald. The guy is versatile with his killing, he doesn't have to shoot someone."

"When did DeLucci take over?" Bruce said.

"A few weeks ago. All went smoothly, and Moroni accepted retirement," Fisher said. "I think you broke the camel's back when you dropped off Dobbs. More Moroni involvement."

"With everyone dead, and the gate locked, how were these killings discovered so soon?" Kate said.

Glenn Mathews

"The housekeeper's daughter called the police when she couldn't reach her mother at home in the evening, or where she worked. No one answered the Moroni phone, so the police obtained a search warrant."

"And, of course, nothing to tie these murders to DeLucci," Bruce stated caustically.

"That's right, nothing yet. But we'll get him. We'll get him," Fisher said. "Damn. If Moroni was alive, just a few more days, he'd be in jail. Or, at least, I would have got an indictment."

"What?" Bruce sat up.

"Kate, this evidence is what I wanted you to also know about," Fisher said. "I don't know how to soften this information, but it needs telling. Thanks to your dad, we got proof on Moroni. We found his fingerprints on several out of the way places in the trunk of the car that brought him here. He placed those prints deliberately. Plucky little guy. We got his finger --"

Kate stood. She began to cry. She hurried toward the bathroom. "I want to hear the rest of this. Wait until I get back," she blubbered.

The two men sat quietly. Each glanced at the other.

Fisher shrugged apologetically at Bruce. He whispered, "Does she still not know about Homer and the --"

"She knows nothing. Let's keep it that way," Bruce said.

"Good."

Kate returned. "I hope I can hear the rest of this. I want to hear it."

"Not much more to tell," Fisher said. "We knew your father was in the Navy during World War Two, and we requested his prints from the naval department. That's how we got a match for several different fingers. Roundabout, but we tracked ownership of the car to Moroni. Plenty to go after him. But, he's dead. We're still working on the car, but without Moroni I can't foresee DeLucci's involvement, or getting evidence on a crime syndicate. Your father's killing will be considered a domestic crime. You know the type. Ex-husband has ex-father-in-law killed for

172

personal revenge. But, if he was alive, he would have talked. Close. Close." Fisher shrugged. "We work on DeLucci now."

After Fisher departed, Kate and Bruce took a walk. The dogs were with them, each on their leash. They wanted to be together, to hold hands, and to smell the fresh air. Ten at night can be chilly in mid-June, but the air was balmy and the moon was full, and appeared so very close.

"Look at the moon, sweetheart," Bruce said. "It's enormous."

"I know," she said, and squeezed his hand. "The moon always seems larger here. That's why this valley is named 'The Valley of The Moon'."

They walked to the town square, through the park, and on the business streets looking at displays in the windows. There was little talk, but relief, contentment, love, and friendship enveloped them.

When they returned Kate put a casette of instrumental music in her stereo. They sat on the sofa holding hands and listened to music for several minutes.

Bruce broke the silence. "I love you," he said softly. "And I want to marry you. Will you marry me?"

"Yes, my darling, I'll marry you," Kate said. She paused for a moment. "But I can't marry you right now. I have to wait awhile. I --"

"I think I know how you feel." He kissed the back of her hand.

"Let me try and explain," she said. "I have spent so many years married, and including my life since the divorce, waiting for something to happen. Waiting for something that shouldn't happen, happen. During my marriage, I had to contend with anger, hate, adultery, an irresponsible and thoughtless parent, mental instability, cruelty, and more. Since leaving that man, the hate, anger, and cruelty still existed and affected me, but much more took place, atrocities." She stood and went to the rear door and looked out its window at the darkness. She thought for several moments.

173

"Looking back, I should have left him much sooner, but I was afraid to. He continually threatened me. I was afraid of him, but I have always been more afraid for the children. What would he do to them if we left him? And he knew how to use my fear. If Karen and Eddie had never been born, or, God forbid, if something had happened to them, I would have gone to the police. I knew enough about him and his--, organization, to put him and others behind bars. I don't know if I would have made it to the witness stand, but I would have tried."

She sat and squeezed his hand again, and he felt the moisture. "Now, that he's dead, I feel a great relief," Kate said. "But I don't know if it's real. Is something waiting around the corner? I don't want you committed to my world until I know it's a good world. I have to adjust, believe it or not, to this new life I hope I have. I have to make sure that day in and day out I am going to be happy, and nobody is going to get hurt." She looked at him intensely. "I love you very much and I hope you understand, my darling. And I do want to marry you." She kissed him on the cheek.

He took her into his arms and they kissed for several moments. They separated. "I understand," he whispered. He smiled down on her. "And just how long are you going to need for this-, adjustment?"

She sat back on the sofa. "A few months."

"Longer than a year?"

"Heavens, no!"

"Then let's plan our wedding for next June, a year from now," Bruce said. "We can be engaged for a year. Can't we?"

"Yes. Oh, yes! I like that. I like that very much," she exclaimed.

They kissed.

"Bruce, we, I have to live in Sonoma. The little town, my home, have become a part of me. And my business is getting better. Am I being selfish?"

"No. I like Sonoma. I'll miss Tiller, but nothing is holding me there. I'm the one that's selfish. I won't be contributing very much in this marriage. You have the business, and the home, and I don't have the bucks I once had."

"Stop it," Kate said. "Those three ingredients to the perfect marriage didn't say anything about money or material benefits. Just love, friendship, and commitment."

"I know, and that's what it should be like. But it'll take some getting used to. I'll probably go back into real estate here, although it takes a longtime to build a reputation and clientele," he said. "But I doubt that I will have my own office again." He frowned. "I can't just do nothing."

"Why not? You've earned it! You've worked hard enough in your life. And what about that book you were going to write?" she said.

"Promises, promises."

"Do it!"

"Maybe. I just might do that." He grinned, and they kissed again. "I'm not going to move in here with you. Christy and I will continue to live in Tiller. Eh, how, eh, how are we going to live over the next year? Do you think we might be able to see each other once in awhile?" he teased.

"At least a couple of times," she said coyly. "Let's see now, there's the Red Lion Inn in Redding. My car can go to Tiller. Infrequently, of course. And you can come down for Thanksgiving, --"

"Christmas, and New Years', and Easter, and horse racing. And if no one but you lives here, and no one is visiting, I just might stay --"

"Overnight in the upstairs bedroom with Selma," Kate interrupted.

They laughed heartily. They enjoyed laughing together. They were in love.

Chapter Twenty

Oregon. June, 1993, one year later.

Bruce was busy getting ready to go. He was a few pounds heavier than the year before, the hair was a little grayer, but just as full. He felt stronger than ever and thought he looked very good in his new dark blue wedding suit that he would be wearing soon.

The river was at its lowest ebb of the year and looked inviting, and the weather was cooperating, not a cloud in the sky, and warm. George was almost packed. The shed was empty. Everything that Bruce had brought to Tiller was either discarded or packed for traveling. He knew that a few things still needed doing. He had phoned the satellite people and cancelled his station service for the next day, but he still had to disconnect the equipment. He would do that in the morning. He had to hook up the trailer to George and disconnect utilities in the morning. Kate and Sally would be arriving in a few hours. Her unpacking won't take that long, including Sally's bed and food, the food being different from Christy's.

Bruce thought about Christy again. He was worried about her. She had deteriorated the past months. He looked out the trailer window and saw her lying nearby. Her breathing was rapid, and she continually panted despite no exercise. She was thinner, having difficulty keeping her food. Arthritis in her hip was very bad, and a tumor was getting larger on her lower gum. Her eyes showed pain. Thirteen was getting up there for a dog, but he hoped she could be around for a few more weeks. Sally and Kate were coming. He hoped she would have some fun on the trip.

Bruce began to smile when he thought about the dogs. He and Kate had laughed thinking that they were the only couple ever married who took their dogs with them on a honeymoon. Most people would probably think they were crazy. She had to bring her car to take Sally. Kate said that no way was Sally going on any airplane, and she had to bring a lot of stuff up here and the car would be more convenient.

They agreed on a trailer trip, leaving Kate's car on the trailer pad. They wanted privacy, to travel some, not too many people in the area, and they wanted to be in pretty country. After Medford, and the brunch, they would go to Loon Lake for a few days. They would travel the Oregon coastline and visit some parts of Washington. They would return to Tiller and Kate would drive her car back to Sonoma with Bruce not too far behind her. The trailer was to be stored near Kate's home. Nothing elaborate, but something they both wanted, and their dogs could be with them.

Bruce was excited, but nervous. He wanted to make sure everything was covered. He got out his list, and his thoughts were rapid. The phone will be disconnected, the electric, got all the food they would need for awhile, the wedding license is in the drawer over there, laundry and cleaning done, cash on hand, and the little church in Medford reserved for eleven in the morning. They would be out of here by eight-thirty in the morning, in plenty of time to greet family and friends. All the kids were coming into Medford Airport at ten, including Jan and Alex, and Billy's coming, and a couple of Kate's friends. Nothing big, a simple ceremony, then a wedding party and brunch at the Jacksonville Inn. By two-thirty, we'll be on our way to Loon Lake.

There was a light tap at the door near the front of the trailer. Surprised that Christy wasn't barking, Bruce opened the door, and grinned. Kate and Sally stood outside the door, and Christy stood, tail wagging.

He thought he had never seen Kate look more beautiful. Her face looked fresh and younger, and her soft brown hair, still cut short, glowed with perfection. She wore brown cotton slacks and a short sleeved yellow blouse.

"You certainly made good time," he said. "I didn't expect you for at least a couple of hours. Come on in."

177

Kate and Sally came inside the trailer. Christy stayed outside. Bruce kissed Kate lightly on the mouth. "I love you."

"I love you," she said.

"You look wonderful," Bruce said. "So pretty, and clean, and fresh." He looked at Sally. "You both just sparkle!"

"How is Christy?" Kate said.

"About the same, sweetheart. I'm just not up to putting her to sleep. I can't do it right now." Tears came to his eyes.

"I know," Kate said.

The telephone rang. Bruce started for the bedroom.

"Darling," Kate called softly to him.

He stopped and looked back at her. She stood in the kitchen by the dinette table. "I love you always," she said. "And, we'll be waiting."

The phone kept ringing. "I love you, too," he said. "I'll get the phone. I'll only be a minute." He turned, went to the bedroom and picked up the receiver. "Hello."

"Dad? Dad. Oh, my God, how do I tell you?" David said. He sounded on the verge of tears.

"David, what's the matter? You sound terrible. What is it?"

"Dad, Kate is dead. Her car went out of control near Red Bluff. Rolled over several times. I'm so sorry. I'm so sorry! She and Sally are dead." David began to quietly cry.

"That's ridiculous. Someone is playing a cruel, sadistic joke on you," Bruce said angrily. "Kate is here. Right here. With Sally, now."

"That's impossible, that's just not possible. Eddie called me a minute ago. The Highway Patrol contacted him. Please, I know this is a terrible shock, but you're not helping yourself by thinking --"

"You can talk to her, yourself. Wait a minute," Bruce exclaimed. He held the receiver, turned, and looked down the interior of the trailer.

No one was there.

He set the receiver down and went to the front door. He stepped outside.

178

"Kate, I --"

There was no one on the patio.

He walked around the trailer. "Kate? Kate? Sally? Christy? Christy," he called softly.

No one came.

Kate's car wasn't out front. He began to panic. He went to the shed. He walked all over the yards. He went along the river. His voice grew louder, and more insistent.

"Kate, Kate, Christy, Sally," he called.

There was no response.

He retraced his steps, calling.

He walked along the road, a half mile in each direction, calling. He looked in gutters and ditches, and along riverbanks.

He found nothing.

He was very tired, near exhaustion. He was not able to call anymore, and his chest began to hurt.

Head down, tears on his cheeks, he returned very slowly to the trailer. He lay on the couch. He couldn't think clearly.

He became aware of a buzzing sound. He went to the bedroom. The phone receiver was making a noise and he replaced it.

The phone rang.

Bruce picked up the phone and held it to his ear.

"Bruce? Bruce? Is that you?" William Fisher said. "Bruce? If you can hear me, just listen. David got hold of me. It's true. Goddamn it, it's true. Kate is gone. Car crash near Red Bluff. Bruce?" Fisher paused. "Your boys are coming up. They're on a flight, and will be with you in about three hours. They'll rent a car in Medford." Fisher paused. "Did you hear me? Your sons will be there soon. Bruce?"

"Okay," Bruce sobbed.

Chapter Twenty-One

The time was nearly eleven when David and Steven arrived at the trailer. David had aged and looked older than his thirty-two years. He had lost weight and the waistline was more becoming. Steven had gained some weight and the extra pounds complemented his tallness. He still looked to be in his mid-twenties. His face registered extreme sadness.

The yard light was on but the trailer was dark. They turned on a light in the living room and kitchen. They looked for their father.

Steven was on the patio.

"There he is." He pointed toward the river. "He's sitting by the trail to the river. On a patio chair."

They went to Bruce. David took his hand. Bruce looked at his son's face and he began to cry, and sob, his shoulders and chest heaved. He stood and David put his arms around him and they held each other tightly.

Bruce saw his younger son, and he went to him, and they held each other.

"I'm sorry," Steve said. "I share some of your sorrow. Kate was a wonderful person. I'll miss her." Steve began to cry.

They walked to the patio. Bruce unfolded the patio chair and sat on it again. "I'd like to stay out here for awhile. Kate and I always enjoyed sitting here. We would sit out here at night, like this, and hear the water." He cried softly.

Steve sat next to him.

"How about a hot cup of tea," Dave said. "And something to eat?"

"I'd like a cup of tea, and there's some doughnuts in a drawer by the refrigerator. I'm sure glad you guys are here," Bruce said.

David went inside the trailer. Bruce and Steven sat quietly together. Several moments passed.

"I'm so happy that you and Karen are married," Bruce said quietly. "Kate was pleased, too. We had fun at your wedding and reception in April."

"Kate helped us out with all that. She really made it a great day for us." Steven shifted his weight.

"Karen helped, too, I'm sure," Bruce said.

"Oh, yes." Steven nodded.

"Is your apartment finished, yet?" Bruce said.

"Just about," Steven said. "We're anxious for you to see it. Karen has great taste in furnishings. A two bedroom, you know, so you'll spend time with us. Sierra Madre is not too far from Arcadia and Santa Anita Race Track." Steve paused a few moments. "Karen sends her love. She wanted me to be sure and tell you that she loves you."

"I'm glad. How is she taking this?"

"Pretty rough. She and her mom were very close."

"You should be with her," Bruce said.

"No. She wanted me to be with you. She insisted."

"Has she gone to Sonoma?"

"Yes. Eddie went with her," Steve said. "He wanted me to give you a hug. Okay?"

"Yeah, consider it done." Bruce tried to smile. "Are they going to make arrangements?"

"Yes."

"When is Karen going to get her teacher's credentials?" Bruce said.

"In August. She's already making inquiries for a job. She wants to teach English in high school," Steve said.

Dave came with a television tray holding a pot of tea, a mug, and a box of doughnuts. He set the tray by his father, filled the mug with tea, and opened the package of doughnuts. David took one doughnut, gave one to his brother, and sat.

"Is that all you want?" David said to Bruce.

"Fine. Thanks, Dave. I always liked English, Steve." Bruce became thoughtful. "Is Kate going to be cremated?"

181

"No, they're going to pick out a casket. And Karen and Eddie want a date that's agreeable with you, Dad. But I think the funeral ought to be in four or five days," Steve said.

"Anytime," Bruce said.

"Let's stay here for a couple of days," Dave said. "We want you to try to rest and relax a bit."

"All right."

"We're going to take the trailer back with us. After the funeral, we'll all go to Southern California. We want you to stay with us," Dave said.

"All right."

"Are you feeling okay, Dad?" Dave said. "I mean health wise, physically. You look very pale."

"I'm all right. My chest hurts some," Bruce said.

"In the morning, we go to the hospital in Medford," Dave said. "You don't look well, Dad. With those chest pains, you need an examination."

"No, I am not going to Medford, or any hospital. Not now," Bruce said.

"You've had bypass surgery," Steven said. "If your chest hurts, you've got to go."

"Listen to me, both of you," Bruce said. "I am not going to any hospital." He was angry and excited. "Later. I'll rest a couple of days here. I want to go to Sonoma. I want to see her." He almost hollered. "Do you understand me?"

The brothers glanced at one another.

David shrugged. "All right, Dad. But when we get home, you get a physical. Okay?"

"All right. Stop worrying about me." Bruce waved his hand.

He looked out at the lighted yard, and he became thoughtful.

"I want you boys to know that when I die I want to be cremated. And if it's all right with Eddie and Karen, I'd like my ashes buried on Kate's grave site."

"Karen and Eddie won't object, and Kate would have wanted that," Dave said.

"Yes. There'll be no problem. That's the way it should be," Steve said. "But you've got a lot of living left."

"I'm going to tell you what happened here just before you called, Dave, and then I don't want to talk about this anymore," Bruce said. "You're not going to believe me. Nobody will, but it's true. It happened." He stopped talking. His face was tired, and very sad. "Do you think Kate's body is in Sonoma yet?"

"I don't know," Dave said.

"Kate and Sally arrived about four this afternoon. Christy greeted them. I kissed her. She looked wonderful," Bruce said. "She asked about Christy, and I told her what she already knew. The phone rang. That was you, Dave. She told me that she loved me, and then I answered the phone." He became quite pensive.

"No, that's not quite right. She told me that she would always love me. And she said, too, that they would be waiting for me. Yes. Yes. That they would be waiting for me."

"Where was Christy when this happened?" Steve said.

"Here, on the patio." Bruce began to weep. "I looked all over for them, but I couldn't find them."

"Are you sure you didn't take Christy to the vet?" Dave said.

"She didn't go to any vet. She was going with us."

"But where is she?" Steve said gently.

"Don't you see?" Bruce stared at them. "Kate didn't want me to put her to sleep. She knew how I felt. She knew how hard it would be for me. Kate and Sally took her."

The brothers looked at each other. Worry and sadness were on their faces.

The next day, the phone rang at ten in the morning. Dave answered. "Hello," he said.

"I think so, Mister Fisher. Hold on a minute. Dad, it's Mister Fisher."

Bruce took the phone, cupped the receiver, and went out the back door to the patio. "Billy?"

"Yes, Bruce. How are you feeling? Did you get any sleep?"

"Some. They killed her. Didn't they?"

There was no response.

"I wasn't going to tell you," Fisher said. "You've had enough already."

"Wasn't hard to figure, Billy. I heard of no other cars involved. Kate was a very good driver. She wouldn't drive over sixty-five on a freeway. She had a newer car in excellent condition. Somebody tampered with it."

"Yes, the steering column. I had a team of mechanics going over it. They checked out that car for hours. They all agreed."

"DeLucci killed her."

"Yes. I'm sure he sent this Gerald. We know that Gerald had eight months of night school in car mechanics when he was eighteen. But, again, no proof."

Bruce began to cry. "Kate wasn't going to say anything. She just wanted to live and be happy."

"I know, my friend."

Chapter Twenty-Two

June, 1993.

The truck and trailer traveled south along the slower lane of interstate 5 at fifty-eight miles per hour. David drove the Suburban.

"Keep it under sixty," Bruce had told Dave earlier. "Fifty-eight miles per hour is tops. Old George was young once, but not anymore, and he's pulling a lot of weight."

"Dad," Steven said suddenly. "What really happened to Christy?"

Bruce turned his body on the seat and looked at his younger son in the backseat.

"I've told you all I can, son," he said sadly.

"What about the road in front of the RV pad? Could she have gotten run over? Did you look in the gutters up and down the road?" Steve said.

"She was taught to stay out of the road and she did. And, yes, I looked everywhere."

"Then she had to drown in the river, Dad," Steven said quietly.

"Goddamn it," Bruce screamed at the dashboard. "She didn't drown! She wouldn't go near the water the last couple of months. She knew better. Now, shut the fuck up!" He breathed heavily for several moments before he seemed to relax. His right elbow was on the armrest and the right hand was over his brow. In a few moments, he started to cry. "I told you what happened," he said quietly. "I told you what happened."

David quickly glanced toward the backseat and looked directly into his brother's eyes. He shook his head.

Two hours later, they approached the northern boundary of Redding, California. Bruce was asleep. David talked quietly to his brother. They heard a siren. David looked at the side mirror and saw the flashing lights of a highway patrol vehicle.

"I wonder if this bastard is going to give me a ticket for going three miles over the speed limit. For Christ's Sake!" David said.

Pulling a trailer over was not the easiest maneuver, and David wanted to make sure they were safe from passing traffic. A wide spot in the road appeared ahead and the rig gradually came to a stop. David rolled down his window and waited for an officer.

The black and white car parked in front of the Suburban. A uniformed officer got out and came to David's side of the truck. He was six foot, two hundred pounds, rugged, dark glasses, and polite.

"Is there a Mister Bruce Campbell in this vehicle?" he said.

Bruce was awake.

"I'm Campbell," he said sleepily. "What have I done?"

"Nothing, sir," the officer said. "Please, all of you relax. I stopped you, Mister Campbell, so that I could bring you to our office in Redding. There's a message waiting for you there from a friend. The same friend who gave us the license and description on this trailer."

Bruce slowly got out of the Suburban. "Get yourself some lunch, and I'll join you there later," he said to his sons.

"And just where the hell is that going to be?" David said caustically.

"Officer," Steven said. "Can you recommend a place where we can get a sandwich?"

"Yes. About five miles ahead there is a turnoff called Lake Avenue. Take it, go to the stop sign, make a right and look for Carl's Jr." The officer pointed. "There's parking for a rig like this and I'll bring Mister Campbell there in less than an hour."

"Thank you," Steve said.

David turned to his brother. "We could stay here and eat in the trailer. There's plenty in the fridge."

"I wouldn't do that, sir, too dangerous," the officer said. "You're very close to the highway here."

"We'll go to Carl's Jr. Thank you," Steve said.

The officer opened the door to his patrol car for his passenger.

They watched their father sit down, the door close, and the officer get into the driver's seat. The car moved cautiously onto the highway but within seconds the vehicle was at top speed, lights flashing, siren blaring.

"This is the damndest trip I've ever been on," David said.

"I agree with you," Steven said calmly. "But very interesting."

Bruce was escorted into Captain Schroeder's office. The Captain was a fat man, short, heavily wrinkled and tanned, in his early sixties. His uniform was spotless but he appeared to be uncomfortable. His belly protruded, the belt inundated with fat. He had a kind face.

"I hope we haven't startled you, Mister Campbell," he said.

"You have, but I'm alright now." Bruce smiled as he sat. "I'm sure there's a good reason."

"Yes, I guess so," Schroeder said. "We received an express envelope this morning from a Mister William Fisher, the district head of the FBI in San Francisco. I opened it and inside was a smaller envelope. Your name was on this envelope with a note to me attached to it." He handed Bruce a business envelope with his name on it.

"The note was from Mister Fisher asking me to phone him in San Francisco. When I phoned Mister Fisher, he told me that he wanted you to have this envelope, the contents being very personal. He thought that you would be driving through this area late this morning or early afternoon on your way to Sonoma. He gave me descriptions and license numbers on your rig. I told him that if you were on the road, and you were, we would have no trouble finding you. The rest you know."

"Yes, and thank you, Captain. May I read this here?" Bruce said.

"Surely." Schroeder stood, walked quickly around his desk and left the room. He quietly closed the door.

187

Bruce examined the envelope. Billy's bold handwriting was evident. He slowly opened the envelope and removed the contents, a small note attached to a larger enclosure. He read the note and the enclosure. He reread them. He gradually replaced the contents in the envelope, folded the envelope in half, and placed it in his shirt pocket. He stared at the floor for several moments. A slight smile appeared. A tear trickled down his cheek, then another. He removed a handkerchief from his rear pocket and wiped his eyes and cheek. He stood and went to the outer office.

Captain Schroeder approached him. The officer who brought him was there. "Is there any response?" Schroeder said. "Anything we can do?"

"No, no, there's nothing to do." Bruce looked at each man. "Thank you. Thank you both, very much."

There was an awkward pause. "Well, I guess we better get you to Carl's Jr.," the officer said.

"That would be nice," Bruce said.

The brothers had a quiet booth and ate their Westernburgers. Each had also ordered large fries and a super coke. They ate in silence.

"This is the first time in a couple of days that at least one of us hasn't been around Dad," David said. "It's a nice relief." He paused thoughtfully. "I guess I shouldn't say that but since the phone call everything that's happened has been so unreal, and I'm worn out with worry and concern. Dad's not well. Perhaps mentally, too."

"I know." Steve ate a fry. "But Dad just needs some rest and he'll begin to remember things differently."

"I doubt that," Dave said.

"Do you want me to have him first?" Steve said.

"No. You've only been married two months. You don't need Dad with you right now. He's all mixed up and that's not helping both of you to adjust to married life. Jan and I'll take him for a few weeks, and little Alex will be a comfort to him. He sure loves his grandson and they get along real well. You guys come over whenever you want. He'll need to see you."

"He's my responsibility, too, and I want him to come and be with us for a few months," Steve said.

"I know that, and he will," Dave said. "But for now, let me have him. I can park the trailer on the driveway for a couple of weeks before storing it, and he can adjust gradually to being without it. Jan's not working and she can keep an eye on him."

"He should be in a hospital," Steve said seriously.

"I agree," Dave said. "But with his attitude, he'd die getting there."

"He'll probably want to return to Tiller, and that could be soon," Steve said.

"Maybe, but he was very willing to pack up and come home with us." David looked out the window and saw his dad get out of the patrol car. "Look at him. He acts like he's ninety years old. He seems so different to me now, yet I love him just the same. Maybe even more. He needs us."

"I know," Steve said. He paused. "Hey, Dad is just tired, very tired, and he needs to rest and relax for a while. He'll be alright."

"I hope so."

"Do you believe what he's told us?" Steve said quietly. "About Kate, and Christy, and all?"

Slowly, David shook his head. "What he revealed is all so irrational. Incredible. But I know he believes it."

Their father had a large cup of tea in his hand when he joined them. He took a couple of swallows. "Boy, that tastes good."

"What about some food, Dad?" Steve said.

"Not hungry, son."

The brothers looked at one another.

"You're not eating, Dad. What's the matter?" Dave said.

"Nothing, just not hungry. I'll get my appetite back one of these days."

"How did that cop know where to stop us?" Steve said.

"Billy Fisher told his boss where to find us. Do you remember Fisher?" Bruce said.

"Yes, we saw him at the cemetery last year, your former student, and a big shot with the FBI now," Dave said.

"Yes, and a good friend."

"How did he find us?" Steve said.

"I don't really know for sure, but I can guess. I know what I would've done," Bruce said. "Billy knew that we'd be leaving Tiller. To verify that and to find out when, there are generally two reliable sources in a small town. One is the doctor, the other a postmaster. He probably checked with Diana at the post office. You went in there yesterday, Dave. Didn't you?"

"Yes, to give her your forwarding address." David paused. "And I told her we would be leaving this morning."

Bruce nodded. "You see, something that appears impossible is really quite simple."

"What did Mister Fisher want?" Steve said.

"To give me a message that he felt was very important, and I guess it was. Yes, it was important." He could see that his sons expected more. "The message had to do with events that recently took place that Billy was involved in." A long pause. "Things that you don't need to know about. A friend was helpful. That's all you need to know." He smiled at his sons.

"Is there anything we can do to help? Are there any problems?" Steve said.

"No, not anymore. I am concerned about one thing, however."

"What's that?" David said quickly.

"That you never lose your love for one another." Bruce looked at them. "You two are a couple of hotheads with each other at times, and I never want ill feelings to separate you. Have your disagreements, your arguments, whatever, but never lose respect or love for one another. You two are family. You can't get much closer. Keep it that way."

There was silence for a few moments. Tears welled from Bruce's eyes.

Steven nodded.
"We will, Dad," David said softly.

Chapter Twenty-Three

Two and a half hours had elapsed since they left Redding. The hum of the motor and their speed became monotonous. They neared Dunnigan, a small community off Interstate 5.

Bruce tried to nap, but his chest pain got worse. He dozed fitfully. He decided he couldn't sleep. He stared at the road. He felt the tires going over the regularity of the cracks and asphalt patchwork on the road. He gazed in the distance. A large meadow was to his right, green and lush, and inviting. He saw a woman and two dogs. They were coming closer to them.

Yes, yes, there they were, he thought. Kate. And Christy and Sally were playing close by her. Yes, look. He raised his right hand to point them out and tell his sons. A massive pain came. His head dropped to his chest.

David glanced to his right. "Something's wrong. Check him out!"

Steven moved forward. Bruce's eyes were closed. His chest wasn't moving. Steven felt for a pulse on Bruce's wrist. He placed his fingers on Bruce's neck.

"Dave, I think he's gone." He began to cry.

"There's a rest area. Thank God! I'll try CPR."

They came to a stop. David ran around the front of the vehicle, opened the door and pulled Bruce carefully to the pavement. He worked on him.

"He's gone, Dave." Steven still sat in the backseat.

Two teenagers, an older couple, three small children, and a young couple congregated nearby.

Steven got out of the truck, and went to the group.

"Please leave," he said.

"Who is the guy, anyway?" one of the teenagers said.

"He's our father. Now get out of here. All of you!" His eyes flashed.

They left.

Steve placed his hand on his brother's shoulder. "He's gone, Dave."

"Yeah, he's gone." Dave began to cry. "I'm sure going to miss him."

"Me, too."

The brothers lifted their father off the pavement and placed him on the rear seat. Steve tucked his legs in so he could lay a little more comfortably.

Dave found a small pillow in the back of George and placed it under Bruce's head. He saw a folded envelope in Bruce's shirt pocket. He took the envelope to the front seat. Steve sat beside him.

Dave removed a front page news article from a morning Chronicle that read:

"Mafia Chief Eduardo DeLucci Assassinated With Henchman Gerald Grandinetti," David read aloud. "Sniper bullets found their targets on the streets of New York when --"

David stopped reading. He took the note that came with the article. The note read: 'Bruce, from me to you, pal. Billy.' He handed the article and note to his brother.

Steve read the note, and he nodded. "Karen told me that she thought DeLucci was involved."

"I kind of guessed that's what happened," Dave said.

Steve got out of the vehicle and went to a trash container. He tore the news article and note, and put the pieces in the receptacle. He got back in George, next to his brother.

"Let's get Dad to Sonoma." Dave started the engine and they left the rest area.

"Yes, let's go to Sonoma," Steve said. Tears were in his eyes, but a smile came. "I don't know that they're in Sonoma, but they're together. I feel it."

"Absolutely," Dave said tearfully.

George continued to pull the trailer, and they traveled at fifty-eight miles an hour.

Two miles south of Dunnigan the 505 Freeway to Sonoma branches off Highway 5. Kate and Bruce stood beside the road with Christy and Sally. The couple smiled, and they waved to the truck and trailer that went past them. They waved until the rig was out of sight.

"Come on, darling, lot's to see," Kate said.

They turned and walked toward the foothills. They held hands, and the dogs ran ahead of them.

ABOUT THE AUTHOR

Glenn Mathews has a BA degree from UCLA with a major in political science and a minor in English. He was in the Army Counter Intelligence Corps and an agent during the Korean conflict. Afterwards, he became an owner and trainer of thoroughbred race horses racing at all major California racetracks.

Later he was in real estate for twenty-three years and operated his own office in South Lake Tahoe, California. In 1988, he retired from real estate. A divorce followed in 1991 after a thirty-six year marriage.

He remarried in 1993, and Glenn and Dee live in Sonoma, California, with their Boston Terrier, Suzy. Prior to Suzy, Dee owned a white Labrador and Glenn owned a black Lab. This is Glenn's third novel.